Faerie Tale

The Tamar Black Saga - Book Five

BY NICOLA RHODES

Faerie Tale

IBSN: 978-0-9561495-4-1

In the same series
Djinnx'd
Reality Bites
Tempus Fugitive
The Day Before Tomorrow
Faerie Tale
Anything But Ordinary
Rise of the Nephilim
Pantheon

Author's Introduction

I had fully intended to end the Tamar Black series with "The Day Before Tomorrow" and move on. So much so, that another series was begun and the first part completed before I was persuaded to return to Tamar, Denny and the rest. It is a decision that I have not regretted. There was clearly more to say and I have had a great deal of fun in saying it.

So, with that in mind, this book is dedicated to my daughter Claudia, without whose influence, it would never have existed.

The shortest of the Tamar books, Faerie Tale takes Tamar and the gang in another direction and may be quite properly regarded in some ways as not the fifth book of the series, but rather the first book of the second part of the series. Introducing, as it does, new themes and ideas, not to mention new villains, and appearing, as it does to me anyway, as a new beginning for my old acquaintances.

~Prologue ~

A very long time ago…

A snowy hillside under a bright moon.
The witches gather.
A ring of standing stones.
A low chanting.
The glint of a blade in the starlight.
A slash, a stab, a scream.
Blood splashes on the stones
The witches leave.

Much more recently…

A snowy hillside under a bright moon.
The witches gather.
A ring of standing stones
A low chanting.
The glint of a blade in the firelight.
A slash, a stab, a scream
The blood splashes on the stones.
The witches dance.
The fog gathers.
Figures appear through the mist.
There is laughter.
The witches scream.
The fog clears, the figures have gone.
The witches lie dead under the shadow of the stones.
And this is only the beginning …

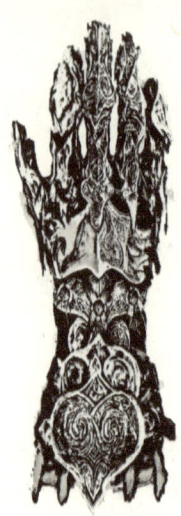

~ Chapter One ~

THE MAN UP ahead in the queue for the cinema was loud, obnoxious and openly and unashamedly sexist. He passed comment, either cruel or lecherous, on every woman who came within his view. It was a situation that was fraught with tension for Denny.

Eventually, as he had known would happen, Tamar could take no more of it.

She poked the man hard in the back to get his attention. 'Do you really think that it's acceptable to talk about women like that?' she queried.

The man just gaped at her. Denny hid his face in his jacket, whether from embarrassment or to hide laughter, it was difficult to say.

'I'm surprised you're still alive,' commented Tamar, ignoring Denny's shaking shoulders (laughing – definitely)

''Ere,' blustered the man – a large bearded rugby playing type with several tasteless tattoos.

Tamar fixed him with a steely eye, but as it happened, he was not addressing her.

'Are you goin' to let your woman talk to me like that?' he demanded of Denny.

Denny composed his features, looked up (a long way up) at this bellicose giant, and said calmly. 'She isn't *my* woman.'

A hurt look passed momentarily over Tamar's face at this disclaimer, but it passed into a smile as Denny continued smoothly.

'She's her *own* woman.'

The man's face relaxed into a knowing sneer. 'First date is it?' he said with deliberate condescension.

Denny turned to Tamar. '*Is* this a date?' he asked her.

Tamar pretended to consider. 'Well,' she said, '*you're* paying,'

'Ah,' said Denny with mock sententiousness, 'then it *is* a date.'

His face clouded and he looked troubled. 'Does that mean that I have to hit him then?'

'Yes.'

Denny sighed. 'Can't *you* do it?' he said, to several shocked gasps from the other cinema goers (well, how were they to know that she was really a Djinn – Genie to you and me – with phenomenal cosmic powers. The result of an ill-advised wish 5000 years previously – oh yes, and immortal too)[*]

'I really can't just go around picking fights with every no-brain who doesn't like the shape of your nose, you know.' Denny added.

'Hah!' she said. 'It isn't the shape of my nose he doesn't like. It's the cast of my opinions.'

'Whatever.'

'Are you going to hit him or not?'

The large man's hearty laughter at this exchange – inspired no doubt at the idea that Denny, who was not exactly an impressive figure to say the least of it, was going to hit *him* – was cut off abruptly as he sailed away on an unscheduled trip to dreamland on the end of an expertly thrown right hook.

'Happy now?' said Denny wringing his hand.

---

[*] See "Djinnx'd" for the full story

'Don't overdo it,' hissed Tamar at Denny's grimacing expression. 'It wouldn't have hurt *that* much.'

(It hadn't actually hurt at all)

'That's all you know,' said Denny *sotto voce*.

'I used to *be* this weedy bloke you see before you.' He reviewed this sentence in his head and added, 'if you see what I mean?'

'And it *did* hurt this much.'

Tamar shrugged. 'You know,' she said, 'all this has put me in the mood for some violence.'

Denny indicated the large cinema poster depicting a picture of "The Rock" looking exceedingly ferocious and waving a bloodstained sword beneath the legend "Cannibal City".

Tamar huffed contemptuously. 'I mean some *real* violence,' she said. 'Let's go and hunt some werewolves.'

'I just wanted a nice, normal evening for once,' thought Denny. 'Why does it always have to end up like this?'

He shrugged helplessly. There was no point swimming against the tide. 'Okay,' he said, 'why not?'

'Well if you don't want to …'

Denny grinned suddenly. 'Nah, it's okay,' he said. 'We should get out of here anyway,' and he indicated the growing throng of people, staring at the scene she had created.

'Yes, just look at the mess you made,' said Tamar. 'I can't take you anywhere!'

* * *

'I just can't take you *anywhere*!' Cindy snapped, and gave the small boy a sharp smack on the legs and dragged him unceremoniously from the supermarket. She strapped him protesting into the car seat as he kept up a steady howl.

'How does he not run out of breath?' she marvelled as his little face turned slowly purple with the exertion, and yet he never stopped.

She drove furiously home, sent him straight to bed, and then began wearily picking up toys that were scattered all over the living room floor.

She had only just sat down to a cup of coffee when a small voice was heard over the banisters.

'I'm sorry,' it said.

Cindy sighed with relief. 'That's all right darling,' she said. 'Why don't you come downstairs then?'

Small footsteps padded down the staircase. He crawled into her lap resting his tiny tear stained face against her blouse. She cuddled him for a moment then he pulled away and looked at her, smiling.

'Will you read me a story?' he asked. The little prince – so secure in his right to be forgiven.

'Of course sweetheart,' said Cindy.

'The one about the fairies,' he demanded.

Cindy nodded and reached for the book. '*A Midsummer Night's Dream*,' she read out.

The boy nodded happily. 'I love you mummy,' he told her.

She hadn't planned on a child. She did not even know for sure where little Jacky's father was now. She had a vague idea that he was in heaven, not dead, but among the angels all the same. Of course, although Eugene had been in mortal form at the time the seed was planted, he had not been exactly human. She wondered what she would tell the child when he was old enough to understand. So far at least, he had not shown any signs of inheriting his father's shape shifting abilities, but perhaps he never would, since those abilities had not been innate to Eugene but rather had been foisted upon him when he had been cast out of heaven. Perhaps Jacky was just what he seemed to be – a normal human little boy. Well, almost …

Her own magical abilities were not natural to her either but the result of decades of hard work and perseverance in learning her craft, a gift of the goddess Hecaté for her dedication.

Hecaté herself now came gracefully into the room and looked wistfully at Cindy and her son sleeping peacefully on the couch together. She still grieved that she had had to give up her own son soon after his birth to a high and lonely destiny, and she, therefore, had been prepared to lavish all the love and attention her thwarted motherhood could muster on this child. But he shunned her and indeed everyone else except his mother. He especially seemed to hate Tamar and, even at two, regarded her with a wary suspiciousness that was altogether unnervingly un-childlike. Jack Stiles (Hecaté's mortal husband) and Denny, he tolerated, but he could not be said to be fond of any of them. And, as he grew older, Hecaté began to feel apprehensive toward him – an unusual emotion for a god.

'How's "The Demon Child"?' said Tamar appearing behind her.

Hecaté jumped and smothered a nervous laugh. 'Do not call him that,' she said.

'Why not?' said Tamar giving the child a look of dislike. 'He is, isn't he?'

Hecaté shrugged. It was difficult to argue with really.

'I don't believe for a minute that kid is really Eugene's,' continued Tamar. 'He was such a nice feller.'

Hecaté looked shocked.

* * *

Tamar threw herself discontentedly into a large armchair. 'I'm so *bored*!' she moaned theatrically.

Denny raised a weary eyebrow – the werewolf hunt had been a disappointment and he was anticipating yet another of her "Sherlock Holmes" type diatribes, bemoaning the serious lack of cunning super-villainy in the world ever since they had buttonholed Askphrit the evil Djinn into his own little pocket universe, where he could do no more harm.

'I mean what's the *point*?' she said. 'What is the point of being a super-hero without a super-villain?'

Denny nodded automatically. He had been down this road with her before.

There had been the sorcerer Thespis, who had been a real let down. Denny had defeated him easily with a length of two by four – hardly a challenge!

They – or rather she – had had high hopes, however, of Smiling Larry Simple who talked to God on a big red telephone and had had big plans to end the world (which unfortunately, had relied on a, somewhat erroneously, predicted Second Coming)

And sundry others of course – none of whom had turned out to have the essential combination of insanity, genius and unlimited ambition that go to make up a true super-villain. (Although Thespis had had the maniacal laughter down a treat)

It was not as though she missed Askphrit always trying to kill them – *she said* – but wouldn't it be nice if *someone* out there would at least present a *challenge*! All she wanted – she said – was a villain with a bit of originality. A *proper* super-villain. 'I should say the world is lucky that *I* don't turn to crime!' she added.

'I should say so,' said Denny emphatically.

But Denny disagreed with the general thrust of Tamar's desire to find a replacement maniac for the not-at-all lamented Askphrit.

'I hardly think you would find many decent citizens to agree with you,' he ventured mildly, unconsciously echoing that other famous sidekick – Dr Watson.

'Well, I suppose I ought not to be selfish,' admitted Tamar reluctantly. 'I guess the world's better off for it and it's only the poor unemployed super-hero who's out of luck.'

'Natural disasters?' offered Denny.

'Snah!' snorted Tamar. 'Too easy.'

'*Easy*!' said Denny. But he let it go. He had had this argument too often lately, and there was no reasoning with her when she was in this mood.

It had never occurred to Denny that Tamar's obsessive behaviour might have its roots in something else – like their now more or less indefinitely postponed wedding. Which had been cancelled the first time due to unforeseen circumstances, i.e. Tamar being kidnapped by a crazed collector,[*] and had

---

[*] These terms are often synonymous

never really been rearranged. 'It's always going to be something' they had realised.

Of course, it might have had nothing to do with it. Tamar was not really the settling down type and, had the wedding gone ahead, (and it was not as if she did not want it to – after all, she loved him) it probably would not have changed her very much. Tamar was a natural fighter and likely to remain so.

Denny himself was all for a quiet life – if at all possible. But the chances were slim to none really. Even without the advent of some maniac trying to take over the world, there were plenty of other, less adventurous, maniacs out there to be dealt with. And on top of them were the aforementioned werewolves, not to mention wizards, witches (the bad kind at least) politicians, gangsters, and the remaining Djinn still to be hunted up. It was not as if Tamar was going to let it go. She never let anything go.

Like that guy in the cinema queue. It was funny really, but Denny thought that kind of thing seemed to be happening more often lately (or was it his imagination?) A definite upsurge in obnoxious behaviour. Nothing dangerous really, nor criminal exactly, just … cruel or mean conduct, like the way school kids could be.

Because of her already low opinion of humanity in general (she conscientiously excepted Denny, Stiles and even Cindy from "humanity" in general) Tamar had not really noticed anything, but Denny's radar was definitely twitching. *Something* was going on, he thought – or might be anyway. At least it was worth keeping an eye on.

* * *

Jack Stiles P. P. I. (Private Paranormal Investigator) London, NY, LA, Aberdeen, (often all at the same time) formerly of Scotland Yard – until he was kidnapped by vampires and lost his job – was noticing a sinister new trend of his own. A larger than normal number of child abductions and all occurring under extremely bizarre circumstances.

Why else, he supposed, would the frantic parents be coming to *him* and not the F.B I.?

Many of the parents reported seeing their baby turning into a bizarre creature before their very eyes and then vanishing. Not the sort of thing you want to report to the police.

Descriptions of these creatures varied immensely, but all the reports had one thing in common. The people who saw the creatures universally agreed that what they saw was evil and was definitely *not* their baby, arguing that the *real* children had already been taken away some time before these creatures were discovered. And who could tell just how long before?

Stiles was, for once, completely stumped. He had no idea what could possibly be going on. He decided to ask Tamar what she thought about it.

* * *

Tamar turned a dull crimson as Stiles related his tale, but, she had to admit, that she had no more idea than he did about what might be going on. Research was more in Denny's line; Tamar was all about the action.

But just let Denny find out who was behind this and point her at them.

'There'll be nothing left but scraps,' she asserted angrily.

Stiles filled them in on the details – such as they were. Only very young children, less than a year old were affected by the phenomenon. Any older siblings seemed to be left severely alone, although many of them were exhibiting strange behaviour. However, this, Stiles thought, could quite reasonably be attributed to trauma caused by the horror of the situation in which they found themselves.

Tamar agreed, 'I think we can dismiss that,' she said.

But Denny was not so sure. 'What kind of strange behaviour?' he wanted to know.

Stiles shrugged. 'I could find out,' he said. 'Do you think it's important?'

'It might be,' said Denny. 'I just don't know. I never heard of anything like this before,' he added.

'Sketches of these creatures might be helpful,' he said now, 'if you can get them. They don't have to be Rembrandts, just a general idea you know.'

Stiles nodded. 'I'll get right on it,' he promised.

Somehow, he felt better now. Tamar and Denny would sort this out. He had never yet seen them fail.

Suddenly a horrible wailing and shrieking was heard from above. Stiles jumped up startled.

'It's okay,' said Tamar. 'It's only Cindy,'

Stiles listened, and the sound resolved itself. She was singing what was, apparently, a lullaby, in a voice more suited to the luring of crows than the lulling of byes.

'S'funny,' said Tamar. 'I mean, it's horrible isn't it? But the brat seems to like it. The only time you ever see it smile is when someone sings – even *that* badly.'

'Hush now my little one – please don't you cry,' Cindy warbled tonelessly.

Denny raised his head. 'I know this one,' he said. 'It sounded better when my mum used to sing it to my brother.'

'To your *brother*?' said Stiles surprised.

But Tamar shook her head warningly. Denny's family relations were not a fit subject for conjecture at the best of times – and this was not the best of times. She wondered at Denny for bringing it up at all.

'She had a lovely voice my mum,' said Denny. 'Voice like an angel – face like a hatchet,' he ended wryly.

Tamar smothered a laugh. 'I guess that's where you get it from,' she said. 'Oh, er – the voice,' she amended hurriedly, 'not the face,'

'Both,' averred Denny mournfully.'

~ Chapter Two ~

DENNY'S SEARCH OF the usual suspects had, so far, turned up few hopeful leads. Trolls were fond of *eating* babies (when they could get them) but there were no records of them transmogrifying *into* babies. And, anyway, the last known kidnap attempt by a troll had occurred more than two hundred years ago and had been unmistakable for what it was. It is hard to mistake a large club-wielding troll for anything else really. Ditto various demon cults, which used babies in the "ritual sacrifices to their filthy gods" – Cindy.

In any case, in no cases of infant abduction, that Denny could find, were the babies *replaced*.

'I get the feeling that I'm not looking in the right place,' said Denny. But he could give no good reason for this assumption, other than "it's just a feeling" and beyond the incontrovertible fact that he had, as yet, found nothing.

'Why replace the babies at all?' pondered Tamar. 'I mean, what's the point?'

'A clean getaway?' suggested Stiles. Tamar nodded uncertainly. It made some sort of sense, but it just did not seem like a strong enough reason for such elaborate precautions.

Denny flatly disagreed. 'It takes powerful magic to transmogrify,' he said, 'and even more to keep it up for any length of time. Why go to so much trouble, when with much less magic, you could teleport the child to the other side of the world if you wanted? *Unless*,' his face brightened, 'you were a shape shifter – but why would a shape shifter want to kidnap children?' Denny's face fell again.

'You know, this whole thing seems familiar somehow,' he said after a minute's thought. 'I feel as if I should *know* what's going on. I'm sure I *must* have read about this *somewhere*. I just wish I could *remember*.' Denny's italics were getting out of hand – a sure sign of stress.

'You wanted to know about the other children,' said Stiles after an awkward pause. 'The ones left behind.'

'Yes?' said Denny.

'Well, according to reports they are all acting mean, you know bullying and teasing other children at school and so on and talking back to their parents. Showing all the signs of being teenage delinquents in training, in fact. Natural signs of stress according to the police psychologists. But I take it you disagree,' he finished, *apropos* of the look that had come over Denny's face.

'The behaviour fits,' said Denny more to himself than to his listeners.

Tamar and Stiles just looked at each other and shrugged.

'Fits with what?' asked Stiles. 'Are you on to something?

Denny was gnawing a fingernail in a distracted fashion and ignored him.

Tamar shook her head and put her hand on Stiles's arm. 'Best just leave him to it,' she said. 'He'll let us know if he's found anything.'

* * *

But Denny did *not* find anything, and the situation was only getting worse. And now there was another problem emerging on the horizon.

At first it did not seem to come within their purview – that is to say it did not seem to be supernatural. Not far from where the large house that they occupied was situated was a village (currently anyway – the house that they all shared moved location frequently – usually when Tamar got bored) and this was surrounded by large areas of dense woodland. So large, in fact, that it could credibly be called a forest. The locals had recently been complaining that a large band of unruly gypsies had taken over the forest and were causing trouble.

At first Tamar and Denny ignored these reports as none of their business, although Cindy had casually mentioned gypsy magic and said that it was extremely potent and powerful when used correctly, but that it was white magic and not to be feared.

However, this seemed to be irrelevant as far as it went, and they all assumed that these were not actual gypsies but rather "travellers" of the sort who roamed around the country in rainbow coloured vans, kept big, ugly dogs, lived on social security and did not bathe.

In view of the complaints of the locals, this seemed a reasonable assumption.

But the incidents were mounting up, and not all of them could be explained away. Most disconcerting was the number of people who seemed to be drawn away into the "forest" – presumably against their better judgement – and, when they returned, claimed that they had no memory of what had happened to them.

Maybe, this *was* their business after all.

'Kidnapped by aliens?' suggested Denny only half jokingly, when this was brought to his attention. (He was a devotee of the "X Files" and he had never yet given up hope that their investigations would bring them into the realm of science fiction.)

He was unanimously ignored.

'Could be hypnotism,' suggested Stiles disinterestedly. He was still concerned with his missing children, and this seemed to him to be a divergence that they could do without.

'To what purpose?' said Tamar.

But Stiles just shrugged. He neither knew nor cared.

'This thing with the kids is really getting to him,' said Denny as Stiles slouched away despondently.

'Not surprising really,' said Tamar.

'No.' Denny looked away and pretended to be absorbed in the newspaper report about the gypsies' latest outrage. They were finding it increasingly difficult to talk about the missing children. He was not terribly interested in the gypsies himself, and could not think of a single reason why they would use hypnotism on the locals – it was probably all hysteria. People got lost in woods all the time, after all.

Suddenly Denny gave a yell of surprise, leapt up from his seat and threw the newspaper to the floor.

'What?' Tamar was startled.

'Shee,' muttered Denny mysteriously enough.

'What?' repeated Tamar.

'Shee, Shee,' he reiterated and pointed to the newspaper. He was becoming incoherent, so Tamar picked up the newspaper and read.

Eventually she said. 'So these people, gypsies, travellers whatever – call themselves the "Sidhe"* so what? That's not a Romany word is it?'

'No, it's damn well not,' said Denny, grim faced and angry. 'It's Celtic, and I think we've just found our child snatchers.

Cindy was in the forest. She had no idea why she had come, but she felt the compulsion to go on even as her reason told her to go back.

But she went blindly on; struggling against the underbrush and low branches that tore at her hair and clothes (she had never been so careless of her appearance before – it *had* to be a spell.) Lured on to a destiny that was both vague and terrifying and yet could not be evaded.

'What do you mean she went into the woods?' Denny's fury was something to see when Hecaté reported Cindy's absence. He did not unleash it very often, and it was all the more effective because of it. Even Tamar was impressed, and Hecaté was downright intimidated. She shrank visibly and Stiles put a comforting arm around her.

---

* The correct spelling but Denny had pronounced it correctly

'It wasn't her fault,' he told Denny belligerently.

'I didn't say it was,' said Denny, nonplussed, 'but we have to find her – it's ... dangerous ... really dangerous out there. I mean you have no idea ...' he trailed off, thinking.

'What is he talking about?' Stiles asked of Tamar, knowing that he would get no answers from Denny now that he was in meditation mode.

But Tamar just shrugged. 'He didn't get a chance to tell me,' she said. 'But I think it has something to do with those gypsies.'

'Not gypsies,' said Denny abruptly.

'No?' said Stiles (the interrogator) 'What then?'

Denny looked sharply at him suddenly and shook his head. 'I'm going after her,' he announced. 'Alone!' he added firmly.

Stiles began to protest, but Tamar thought she understood and came down unexpectedly on Denny's side.

'Oh let him go,' she said lightly. 'It's probably just a wild goose chase anyway. Denny's just got a bee in his bonnet again I expect.'

Denny threw her a grateful look, which did not go unobserved by Stiles. But he held his peace. If Tamar did not care about going, then perhaps it really *was* nothing. It was not like Tamar to shun danger. Not on purpose anyway.

The truth was, of course, that Tamar had remembered Denny's final remark to her about the connection of the gypsies to the child snatchers and had realised that Stiles would not be constrained by any method known to man or demon if he had known this. Better that Denny go alone to retrieve Cindy, since he alone, at this point, seemed to know what he would be getting into. Tamar, meanwhile, would try to find out what on earth had prompted Cindy to do such an uncharacteristic and foolish thing.

Another truth, as yet unknown to Tamar, was that Denny, in fact, had no idea what he was getting himself into. Not that it would have stopped him if he had.

'When did she go?' asked Tamar, realising, even as she said it, that it was now a moot point.

'Not long, I think,' said Hecaté.

'You think?' said Tamar. 'Don't you know?'

'Well,' Hecaté explained laboriously, 'two-year olds have little sense of time you see and so the little one could not tell me how long ago she left exactly. Only that it was before lunchtime …'

'Little one?' snapped Tamar. 'You mean that demon spawn of hers is the only one who saw her go?'

'Do not call him that,' begged Hecaté.

'Did it … did *he* tell you that she went into the woods?'

'Yes.'

'Then,' said Tamar grimly, 'we only have his word for it. And frankly I don't think …'

'Shhh,' said Stiles as little Jacky came toddling into the room with such a look of malevolence on his face as is rarely seen on a child of that age – teenagers, now that's a different thing.

'Where's Mummy?' he demanded, looking at Tamar with no very friendly gaze, as if he suspected her of spiriting her away.

'*You* tell *me* – rug rat,' said Tamar unconcernedly. It was not for her to be intimidated by a rebellious toddler even one with such a look of concentrated evil on his face. It was like "The Return of Chucky" she thought inconsequentially and almost laughed out loud.

'Mummy's gone to the woods,' said the child and smirked in a disconcerting fashion. He looked very pleased about it for some unfathomable reason.

Tamar was immediately suspicious. 'What do you know about it?' she said menacingly. But she did not approach the child, Stiles noticed.

Jacky ignored her, but began to sing softly to himself. 'If you g' down t' the woods t'day, you're in for a big s'pise. If you g' down t' the wood t'day you better g' in di'guise.'

Tamar could have killed him.

Denny caught up with Cindy with surprising ease. She was wandering aimlessly in a small copse that was not more than a mile from the house and yet it felt as if he had left civilisation a long, long way behind him. 'I don't remember the place being like this,' he thought.

The forest (it simply was not possible to think of it as merely a wood when you were in it) was making him uneasy. Although it was only around two thirty in the afternoon, it was as dark as midnight in here, there was a primeval atmosphere and Denny could not shake the feeling that scary, primitive things were lurking in the shadows. The sooner they got out of here the better.

When he called her name, Cindy turned to him with a blank stare as if she did not recognise him.

He strode up to her and shook her by the shoulders. 'Cindy?'

'Mmm?'

'Are you all right? What are you doing out here?'

'Not sure,' she muttered. Then suddenly she focused sharply on him. 'Denny?'

'Of course you nit wit,' snapped Denny, his voice shrewish with relief.

Cindy smiled and suddenly she was beautiful, ethereal. Denny stepped back in shock. Of course, Cindy was attractive – she worked hard at it. But this was something different. As he looked at her, Denny felt his head swim.

'I love it when you do that,' she told him dreamily.

'Do what?' asked Denny knowing full well what she meant but inexplicably wanting to encourage her.

'You know,' she said, 'when you go all masterful.' She gave a deep languorous sigh. 'It's *so* sexy.'

'Oh God', said a little voice in the back of Denny's head, but he scarcely heard it. He brushed her face lightly, and she shivered ecstatically.

'Yeah?' he said. Something was bringing out the greasy rebel in him.*

Her hair was astonishingly beautiful, he realised suddenly. It gleamed a pale gold in the … total lack of sunlight actually. He shook himself, momentarily disorientated. He became vaguely aware of the sound of silvery laughter in the trees. Then he looked at Cindy and forgot everything else.

'Mmm.' She leaned in toward him.

He grabbed her roughly by the shoulders and bent her head back.

She closed her eyes in anticipation 'I always liked you,' she told him.

Denny knew it. But his own feelings had always been somewhat ambivalent toward Cindy; he tolerated her – that was all. And Cindy herself would never throw herself at him like this, she was too proud.

In the end, it was his sense of morality that stopped him. Something was wrong with this scenario. If he let himself be tempted, he would never forgive himself.

Oddly enough, it was not Tamar he was thinking of. Cindy's feelings may be real or not, but his own definitely were not, and he must not hurt her by taking advantage of this situation. He drew back sharply and the world came back into focus. He felt suddenly certain that they were being watched.

'It wasn't real,' he thought.

Cindy's face mirrored his confusion. 'What just happened?' she said.

'It doesn't matter now,' said Denny brusquely. 'Let's get out of here.'

'Where are we anyway?'

Denny opened his mouth confidently and then shut it again abruptly. 'I have no idea,' he admitted eventually.

Cindy rolled her eyes. 'Honestly!' she sniped and Denny felt a strange sense of relief about this. He wondered why.

'You don't remember *anything*?' asked Tamar.

'No.'

---

* All men have a little "rebel" in them

'No.'

Both Denny and Cindy were tired, dirty and fed up, and Tamar's relentless questioning was not helping. Both also felt inexplicably guilty under Tamar's accusing gaze.

'But you were gone for *hours*!'

'I told you, we got lost,' snapped Denny

Tamar was not really suspicious. That was in their imagination; she was, in fact, only extremely worried, and it was making her push them.

'But ...'

At that moment, rather fortuitously, Cindy fainted. Denny had never been so grateful to her.

Then all warm and fuzzy feelings evaporated as Jacky came running into the room with a look of concentrated malevolence on his face and bit him on the leg.

It was surprisingly painful, and Denny fell as his ruptured leg collapsed beneath him. 'What the hell ...?'

Tamar never hesitated. She swept Jacky up in an iron grip and belted him across the face in fury.

Jacky, not unpredictably, began to wail and struggle. The noise brought Hecaté running into the room. She saw Denny and Cindy on the floor and Tamar gripping the screaming Jacky at arm's length with a look of horror on her face, and a terrible fear took hold of her. What had the monster child done? *

'Let him go,' Denny's voice came from the floor. He sounded calm enough, but there was an undertone that Tamar knew well enough to make her suddenly drop Jacky like a hot coal. He scampered away whimpering.

Stiles listened with a grave face as Tamar related what had happened. On the face of it, it would not seem like a serious incident. Infuriated toddlers often bit, but the fact was that Denny had a severe wound that would not heal magically and

---

* Now and then, Hecaté admitted to herself that she was afraid of Cindy's baby

was now sitting with his heavily bandaged leg elevated while the blood continued to flow. He looked pale.

Cindy was in bed and Hecaté was with her, watching her anxiously. No one knew where Jacky was, and Tamar said she hoped he had fallen down the well* and good riddance to him if he had. Neither Stiles nor Denny were inclined to disagree, but it seemed too much to hope for.

The fact was they were all tired, bewildered and confused. Nothing like this had ever happened before. Bad things were clearly afoot – and that was nothing new – but they had no idea what they were or who was behind it or why it was happening. There seemed nothing to get hold of – nowhere to start. It was exhausting just thinking about it.

Something clicked in Tamar's brain. 'Who are the Sidhe?' she asked Denny.

'Not who,' said Denny. 'What.'

'Okay then, *what* are the Sidhe?'

'Traditionally they were a Celtic folk tale – fairies basically.'

'*Fairies*,' spluttered Stiles in disbelief.

'Oh God,' groaned Tamar. 'I think I preferred the vampires.'

'I thought they were gypsies,' said Stiles.

'Perhaps they are,' suggested Tamar. 'Maybe they just sort of borrowed the name – er *Celtic* gypsies.'

Denny struggled to his feet. 'Let's go and find out,' he said.

---

* They did not have a well, this being the 21st century. But you did not argue with Tamar

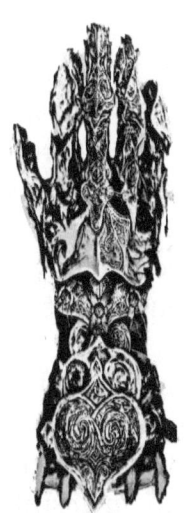

~ Chapter Three ~

CINDY WAS SITTING up in bed watching TV. She was watching Teletubbies because Jacky had returned and was sitting beside her looking unimaginably smug. Hecaté was standing in the doorway watching him cautiously.

He was singing softly under his breath. 'If y' g' down' t' th' woods t'day ...'

Hecaté turned away.

'Hey,' shouted Jacky suddenly, 'whe' you goin' lady?'

Hecaté summoned her courage, she was a *goddess*, she told herself. 'I am not afraid of you,' she said.

'Oh yes you are,' asserted Jacky.

'You just watch out,' said Hecaté. 'Tamar will deal with you, you shall see.'

'Not her,' said Jacky. 'That nasty lady she nev'r comin' back now. She gone. They all gone.' And he started to sing again. 'if y' g' down t' th' woods t'day you in f' a big s'prise ...'

Hecaté fairly ran from the room.

It was not Cindy's child. It *could not* be! Not that horrible creature. Hecaté thought about his early babyhood. The others seemed to have forgotten, but he had been a sweet loving little thing for a while. That had lasted only a few months really, but Hecaté remembered. So what had happened?

'Denny would know,' she mused, 'if only he were here.' She shivered, the house seemed so cold and empty without the others, and she felt alone and vulnerable trapped in the house with that thing. 'Denny would know,' she reiterated, and then – 'Denny *did* know.' She just had to find his notes.

They had been walking through the densest part of the woods for several hours, when they saw the lights. (They kept calling it "the woods" even though the primeval rainforest atmosphere remained, even intensified – it made them feel better) It was lush, verdant and superficially beautiful, but so terribly menacing that even the usually imperturbable Tamar felt the fear growing in her. They walked in a haze of uneasy loveliness, and had no idea where they might be going. Tiny pinpricks of lights danced like a swarm of fireflies away in the distance glowing green.

'Like the matrix,' said Denny to general disdain. But when he commented that he felt like an unwanted intruder on a distant world, neither Tamar nor Stiles disagreed with him, they knew what he meant. They all felt very far from home. The familiar woods had become an alien place, filled with ominous lights and shadows. There was no sound apart from their own voices and the soft tread of their feet.

And the feeling of being watched, which had been growing on them for some time, intensified. But as they walked toward them, the lights seemed to recede and fade then spring up somewhere else.

It was five O' clock on a winter's evening, so the sun was going down above the trees somewhere no doubt, although they could not see it, and yet in contradiction of all likelihood, the darkness did seem to increase further.

And yet, the air remained oddly warm and muggy and the ground was muddy beneath their feet, there was no sign of the frostiness that they would have anticipated had they thought about it, but all rational thought seemed to slip away from them and collapse into nervous anticipation. The trees overhead dripped as after a rainstorm, and it was hard to breathe.

Denny was limping badly, but the inner strength borrowed from the Athame[*] that he always carried kept him going.

Still, Tamar was worried; it had been a long time since she had seen him like this. And, despite her own considerable powers, she had been unable to help him. What kind of a thing had the power to do this?

Well, that was what they were going to find out.

They continued walking for another half hour without seeing anything except the lights, and then Denny collapsed.

Without warning, several people appeared from behind trees. They looked normal enough, but Tamar and Stiles instinctively formed a defensive barrier between the fallen Denny and the newcomers.

'Don't come any closer,' warned Tamar and the intruders fell back nervously.

There were three women and two men all looked extremely bedraggled and dirty. One woman started to wring her hands and a man clasped her by the shoulders protectively.

'I think they're harmless,' said Denny from the ground. 'In fact, I think I know some of them.'

Tamar peered more closely at them. 'They're from the village,' she said in surprise. She addressed the man nearest to her. 'What are you doing out here?' she said.

'Gypsies,' the man said hoarsely.

'Where?' snapped Stiles in panic looking around him.

'No, no, said the man. They sent us to get you. It's not safe out here.'

'They've been looking after us,' volunteered a woman. 'We wandered in ... wandered and ... I ... I can't remember.'

---

[*] A demonic dagger that confers supernatural powers on the owner. In Denny's case, the powers of a Djinn stolen from Askphrit– see "Reality Bites"

'Don't know how you got here?' asked Stiles, and Tamar nodded shrewdly.

'Couldn't find our way back,' resumed the man.

'Couldn't the gypsies have helped you?' asked Stiles.

'They're stuck too,' he replied. 'But at least they're all together. 'You come with us now,' he glanced at Denny. 'We brought a stretcher,'

Tamar and Stiles walked a little way behind the procession carrying Denny.

'Do you feel it?' Tamar said. 'Something's wrong.'

'How did they know that Denny couldn't walk?' said Stiles.

'Crystal ball?' said Tamar dismissively. 'But the air feels wrong, thick and heavy and it's too warm, I don't like it.'

'Then you think these are *real* gypsies then?'

'Probably. We'll soon know,' answered Tamar, in a voice that let Stiles know that the subject was closed.

'I feel like I'm being watched again,' noted Stiles, in reference to Tamar's earlier comments.

'Yes, but it's more than that,' she said. 'I feel like someone's reading my mind.'

As they crossed the invisible border into the gypsy camp, everything in the forest felt different. The air was sharp, clear and cold. The ground under their feet crunched, and the trees were rimed with frost. It was like passing into another country.

The gypsies were welcoming. It was like a small court really. Despite the tattered tents and dirty faces, there was a certain tawdry grandeur about the place, a kind of stateliness. A certain decorum was followed and a loose hierarchy appeared to exist. And all this was presided over by a ragged yet colourful king, who had a face like a piece of carved teak (yet the features were more like those usually found carved in marble) perfect manners and a tent to himself with gold braiding around the door flap, and his own blanket.

They were fed and placed by the fire to warm them up. Then the gypsies told them what they knew.

They had been living in the forest for some weeks when their people began to disappear and they saw the strange lights in the trees. They knew that the local people were blaming them for the trouble because lately several strangers had turned up wandering near their camp and told them so, but they swore they had nothing to do with it.

'It is a power far older than ours,' they said. But they did not know what it was.

So they had fenced themselves in with spells and charms and, so far, it seemed to be working as long as they kept their vigilance. Sometimes people tried to leave the camp but were always stopped, and the strange lights never entered the camp at night now, but the gypsies were worried that they would not be able to hold them off forever.

'We might ...' began Tamar but was nudged into silence by the ever-suspicious Stiles. She had been about to say that they might know what the lights were, but Stiles reminded her to trust no one at this stage. As far as he was concerned, it was either a remarkable coincidence that these "gypsies" had turned up at exactly the same time as all the other trouble had begun, or else they were, at the very least, not telling them the whole truth. If it was not an absolute tissue of lies from beginning to end.

Fortunately, no one seemed to have noticed that she had spoken.

The gypsies did have a name for the strange lights in the forest. "Sidhe".

'I thought the gypsies *were* the Sidhe,' said Tamar a little later, as they sat apart at the edge of the campfire.

'No,' said Denny. 'We just assumed it because of the way the newspaper article was worded. It never actually said as much. It talked about "gypsy outrages" and then later mentioned the name Sidhe as the one people mentioned when they returned'

'So, it's a coincidence?'

Stiles snorted sceptically.

Tamar nodded. She did not think so either.

Later that night, around midnight, when the camp was silent, Tamar was filled with a sudden urgent desire to wander into the forest. Why, she could not have said, even if questioned at the time – later she was to be equally uncertain.

Stiles – who was born vigilant – saw her go and silently followed her. He did not wake Denny who, unable to walk, would only have slowed him down.

After she had walked about 400 yards Tamar stopped abruptly and, without turning round, said, 'I know you're there Jack.'

'Damn! I was sure I didn't make a noise,' he thought.

She turned to face him 'I didn't hear you,' she said as if reading his thoughts. 'I just knew. I knew you would follow me.'

She moved toward him slowly. 'And now we're alone,' she said. There was no mistaking her meaning; it was in the tone of her voice. She sounded ... seductive.

Stiles immediately became nervous. 'A-alone?' he stammered. 'Are you sure, that's a good idea ... out here I mean ...?' he gestured vaguely around him.

Tamar was beautiful even by ordinary standards – even by supermodel standards – but Stiles had got used to it by now – or thought he had. Ha! Who did he think he was he kidding?

She was standing completely still surrounded by a glowing eldritch light which made her look oddly fragile (arousing feelings of protectiveness in Stiles that he had never had before in relation to Tamar, who was a girl who could take care of herself) and so beautiful that she took his breath away.

'Better than mortal man deserves?' she said reading his mind again.

'I never saw anything so beautiful,' he agreed. 'I never met anyone like you,' he told her moving closer. 'You're not just beautiful, you're brave and clever and you care, and I think – I think that somehow it shines through. You're beautiful all the way down in your soul, and it shows through. Your beauty really does come from within.'

Tamar raised an eyebrow. Even under the influence of the spell she was surprised at this glowing rhetoric coming from the relatively stolid Stiles, who had probably never said words like that before in his entire life, or even thought of them. Also, she knew that it was all cobblers. Tamar was a tough bitch, and she knew it. But she was moved all the same.

Her head was swimming; the dank and horrible forest had taken on a rosy hue, and she was sure that she could hear the swell of an orchestra. Little birdies were tweeting, and she was vaguely aware of what sounded suspiciously like crashing waves (and they were at least seventy miles from the ocean). There were rose petals.

'There'll be champagne next,' though the tiny cynical core of Tamar that never quite surrendered.

'Jack,' she said softly. Are you saying what I think you're saying?'

'I'm not good enough for you,' he answered.

'I think you are,' she said. 'I always thought you were a remarkable man.'

'Really?'

'Oh yes, and far too modest.'

'I'm getting old now,' he said. 'And I never was handsome even when I was young.'

Tamar denied it. 'Yes you are,' she said. 'Sort of. *I* think so anyway. From what I hear, handsome is as handsome does, you know. And it must be true 'cause look at you.'

'That's just an old saying,' said Stiles.

'Well, if there's even a grain of truth in it, then you must be far handsomer than me,'

Stiles was looking at her uncertainly. 'Do you really mean all this?' he said. 'I mean, it seems like … I dunno. You've never said … I think maybe you don't know what you're saying. I can't … take advantage of you if you're well … not yourself maybe … or … I dunno …' he trailed off.

She smiled. 'Jack …' she reached for him.

'No! It isn't a good idea,' he said weakly. And he untwined her arms from about his neck with shaking fingers.

She pouted irresistibly. 'If you don't want me, just say so,' she said. 'But I know that you do.'

'Tamar …' He put his arms around her. 'I'm sorry,' he said. 'I don't know what I was thinking.'

She kissed him, and the world spun.

He said. 'I love you.'

This was ludicrous, and the spell broke. Tamar pulled back, and they just stared at each other dumbly.

'That wasn't real, was it?' said Stiles eventually, as if he was not certain.

'No!' said Tamar a little too emphatically.

'Only… it kind of *felt* real,' he said.

'You mean apart from the fact that it clearly *wasn't*,' said Tamar acerbically. *Rose petals*!

'Well, yeah, apart from that.'

'You and I don't say those kinds of things, especially to each other.'

'I know,'

'It was a spell. Something got inside our heads and made us say that stuff.'

'I know, but …'

'Yeah, *but* … You tried it on with me once before I seem to remember,' she added.

'And *you* told me that you would have let me, if it wasn't for Denny,' he reminded her.'

This was true.

'So … was it real, or not?' she wondered.

'We'll probably never be sure,' he said.

'Not here,' she said. 'Not with things playing with our heads. We'll know when we get out of here because we *are* going to talk about this when we get home. Until then, this mustn't happen again.'

'Why would it?'

She looked at him meaningfully. 'You know why,' she told him.

'Magic?'

'Chemistry,' she said. 'Now let's get back to the camp and don't let Denny know about this or, injured or not, he'll rip you apart.'

'Know about what?' said Denny

~ Chapter Four ~

THE PROBLEM WITH being a goddess is that you never really learn how to work a computer. I mean, why would you need to? That stuff is for mortals.

Hecaté did not even know how to turn the damn thing on, so she tried a trick that Tamar often employed with recalcitrant technology, and which annoyed Denny no end. She looked sternly at it. The computer came on.

She was so surprised that she shot backwards in the wheeled chair and knocked over a hideous oil lamp that Cindy had acquired from somewhere. Denny had joked that it was her childhood night light from the days before electricity, and it was certain that everybody hated it. It was pottery of some kind – like a jug and had horrible gargoyle type faces moulded onto it. So, when it smashed into million pieces, Hecaté ignored it and began her search on the computer without a second thought.

The method she used to search was similar to the way she had turned the thing on. Since she had no idea what she was looking for, or how to look for it, she merely asked the computer in a firm voice to show her the last files that Denny had been looking at. After what Hecaté took to be a few seconds thought, the computer responded with a face on the screen, which said. 'I'm not a magic mirror you know,'

'Oh sorry,' said Hecaté without surprise. After all, as far as she knew this was how it was supposed to work. 'I'm new at this,'

'Ah well,' said the computer, no harm done I suppose. Everyone has to start somewhere. Would you like a tutorial?'

'Er, not really, I'm in a bit of a hurry today.'

The computer sighed. 'Very well then, the last files, was it? Searching … These files are restricted you know,' it told her suddenly. 'He really shouldn't have downloaded them – he's always doing that you know,' it added conspiratorially. 'Naughty naughty.'

'Doing what?' asked Hecaté, not understanding.

'Hacking the mainframe,' said the computer severely. Hecaté nodded; at least she understood that bit.

'I'm not sure I should show you these really,' continued the computer.

Hecaté considered her options. She could say "please" or she could …

'If you do not,' she said. 'Then I might as well...' she paused dramatically. 'Spill a caffeinated beverage onto you. The computer blinked, and the files came up.

Hecaté read them avidly.

'Oh, no,' she said eventually. 'Not *them*!'

* * *

'Know about what?' repeated Denny looking at their shocked and guilty faces. 'Tamar?'

'Just that I wandered off,' she said unable to meet his eyes. 'Er, we didn't want to worry you.'

'Don't,' said Denny.

'What?'

'Lie to me,' he said, his eyes blazing, his fists clenched.

Then he seemed to relax suddenly. 'You really don't have to,' he said calmly. 'I know what happened here.'

'You're taking it very well,' observed Stiles.

Tamar gave him a furious look, but Stiles shrugged.

'If he knows, he knows,' he said. 'He probably saw everything, and if he wants to kill me, I can hardly blame him. But he's right. We shouldn't lie to him.'

'I don't want to kill you at all,' said Denny. In fact, I know what happened here, because it happened to Cindy and me too. I know you couldn't help it. And I'm guessing you stopped yourself, like I did. Because it's not real, although it certainly felt it.

'We have to be careful,' he continued. 'If you really want to know, I followed you because I had a feeling something weird was going on. But I didn't see anything. I couldn't keep up with you.' He tapped his injured leg. 'I'm glad I missed it,' he added. 'That's probably a memory I could do without.' He gave a forced laugh.

'You said that you couldn't remember anything,' said Tamar accusingly – referring to the aforementioned incident in the forest with Cindy.

Denny shrugged. 'You see?' he said. 'And I suppose you would have told me all about *this* would you, if I hadn't caught you?'

'That's different,' she said without thinking. 'You said you *knew* it wasn't real …' Then she clapped her hand over her mouth, but it was too late.

'But *you* weren't sure?' said Denny. 'I see.' He looked away biting his lip.

'Denny…?' began Tamar, but he just gave her a look, which silenced her. She had never known him so cold.

Denny sat down suddenly as if his leg was giving him pain, and Tamar hurt inside that she could not comfort him – he did not want her right now.

There was a long, awkward silence in which nobody seemed to know what to say.

Eventually Stiles spoke. 'We should get back,' he said

And Denny attacked him.

It was a more evenly matched fight than it would otherwise have been, inasmuch as Stiles was managing to hold his own due to Denny's injury. But he found it hard – as the guilty party – to fight back with any real commitment. He felt he deserved his beating, and frankly, he wanted it. Only his instinctive sense of self-preservation made him defend himself at all, and Denny was beating him down.

'Stop it,' shouted Tamar. 'You'll kill him!'

Denny felt as if icy water had been poured down his back at these words. He stopped and stood up straight looking down in shock and horror at Stiles bloody face. He felt the real world come flooding back into his consciousness. It was true, he realised. Had he carried on he *would* have killed him.

'*That* wasn't real either,' he said suddenly realising the truth.

'None of this is. We have to get out of here,' said Tamar.

'No, we're being manipulated,' said Denny. 'All this, right from Cindy coming down here in the first place, it was all planned. We can't leave yet; we have to find out why.'

'I don't care why.'

'I don't believe you,' said Denny bluntly. 'Of *course* you care, but *something* doesn't want us here, and doesn't want you to care. You have to fight it. You *always* care, remember that! Now heal Jack up and let's go.'

'The Sidhe?' said Tamar bending down to take care of Stiles.

'What?'

'You said *something* doesn't want us here, but we know what it is, don't we? The Sidhe.'

'I don't know what you're talking about,' said Denny.

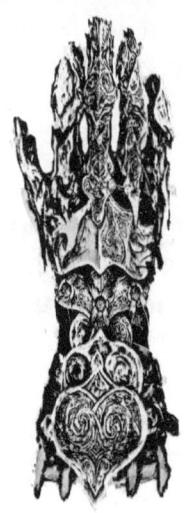

~Chapter Five ~

'FAERIES!' THOUGHT HECATÉ, 'after all this time?' She had seen Faeries before, many centuries ago, and knew well the destruction they could wreak. But she thought that they had all been banished or destroyed or something. However, it appeared that they had only been biding their time. Biding their time until *what*, though? What did they want now? What they always wanted of course, she realised. Entertainment.

'Oh, yes'! she thought. 'They think that humans are toys.'

Watching people make fools of themselves was by way of light entertainment for the Faeries. Like TV. "All The World's a Stage" or rather, in these modern days, a Soap Opera.

But it was worse than that, because they had the power to direct the action.

They had been gone for centuries – or had they? – So, what had happened to them? *Somebody* had dealt with them once.

She realised that she was getting incoherent. Her thoughts were spiralling out of control. It was the panic of course. Tamar, Denny and her beloved Jack were out there in the woods with those things and, what was worse, had no idea what they had got themselves into.

* * *

Tamar did not usually panic, but this was all getting too much for her. She was used to being the manipulator not the manipulated, and if Denny was going to go ga-ga, it was over her dead body. But was he? Or was it her? Did she just imagine that Denny had told her about the Sidhe? Suddenly she was not sure.

'What are the Shee?' said Denny innocently.

'You tell *us*, 'came the voice of Stiles from the ground. You were the one who brought them up in the first place.

'I never ...' Denny trailed off uncertainly.

But Tamar now felt a little better. Obviously, Denny had been got to, which meant that he was probably on to something. Unless ... it was she and Stiles who were the ones ... she shook her head to clear it. It did not help; this was mind control, too subtle a form of attack to deal with directly as per her usual method of solving a problem – hit it and it will go away. Denny was the subtle one. They needed Denny to solve this, and he was "away with the fairies" to coin a phrase. All Tamar's instincts told her to find the Sidhe and beat holy hell out of them until they gave up. But her common sense told her that they would not be found unless they wanted to be, not unless there was some way to free their minds first.

'What's wrong with him?' asked Stiles.

'They made him forget,' said Tamar tersely.

'But not us?' said Stiles. 'Why not?'

'Because we don't really know anything I suppose. He's the one who found out ...'

'We can't believe anything,' interrupted Stiles. 'Not even our own memories. How do we know that he found out *anything*? How do we know that he didn't tell us if he did? I mean maybe he *did* tell us, and we just can't remember it. Or maybe ...'

'There's no point in second guessing ourselves ... do you hear that?'

Faint and distant was the sound of silvery laughter echoing through the trees.

'*Someone* is finding all this very amusing,' said Tamar grimly.

She sent a bolt of lightning through the trees, more to relieve her feelings than anything else, but she was horrified by the result. Instead of the surrounding trees catching fire as you might have expected, the lighting raced up the trunk of a nearby oak and danced through the upper branches crackling from leaf to leaf like a living thing. Then, without warning, a bolt came shooting down from the canopy and struck Denny right in the head.

It did not throw him too far and, once Tamar got over the shock, she could see that he was not seriously hurt, only a little singed and extremely surprised.

'Bloody Hell!' he said

'Are you all right?' said Tamar anxiously.

'Fine,' said Denny. 'Actually, I'm more than fine. I'm me again. Nothing like a good bolt of lightning to clear the brain if you know what I mean?' He winked.

Tamar did see. 'Do me,' she said catching on immediately.

Denny hesitated, on the one hand, he knew, rationally, that it would not harm her in any way, but, on the other hand, there is an inherent cultural taboo against throwing bolts of lighting at your girlfriend, no matter how much she is asking for it.

Stiles was gaping at them in horror. This seemed like the craziest thing yet.

Tamar narrowed her eyes. 'Oh come *on*!' she snapped. 'I want to know that what I'm thinking is what I'm thinking …

'If you see what I mean,' she added after a moment's thought.

Denny struck.

Tamar picked herself up and dusted herself down. It tickles,' she announced blithely.

'And…?' questioned Stiles who had caught up by now.

'It worked,' she tapped her head. 'Clear as a bell.'

'I'm certain,' she added as Stiles looked doubtfully at her.

'It's hard to explain,' said Denny. 'But it's different … you just know.'

'Pity you can't do me then,' said Stiles glumly.

'Maybe just a *little* bolt,' said Tamar. 'Might work. Probably knock you out for a while but ...'

'No!' said Denny. 'Too risky, he's human.'

'More risky than not being in control of your own mind?' said Stiles. 'Do it.'

'It could kill you,' said Denny.

'I'll risk it,'

'Look I just ...'

'Oh, *I'll* do it,' interrupted Tamar. And, before Denny could stop her, she had.

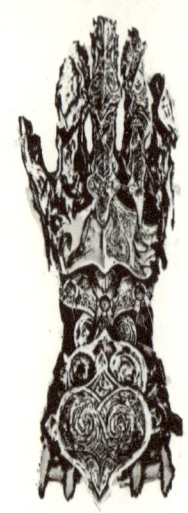

~ Chapter Six ~

THEY WERE HERE many millennia ago. The fair folk, the lordly ones, the Faeries. And in some ways, the land has never forgotten them.

They spawned a million myths and legends and had a hundred different names, but no one remembers the truth.

Vague echoes of the truth have filtered down through the centuries. People talk of mischief, of tricks and pranks. People educated in Faerie lore might mention the courts, the Seelie Court and the Unseelie Court, the homes respectively of the good and the bad faeries.

But there were only ever the bad faeries – only ever the Unseelie Court. And its real name is forgotten.

But Hecaté remembered.

As she ploughed through the many written works that Denny had found on Faeries and their counterparts, recollections of the truth filtered back to her.

They were afraid of iron (iron to bind.)
They loved music (music to maze.)
They were beautiful.
They were elegant.
They were cruel.

They were vicious.
They were murderers.

But she still did not know where they had gone, had never known as a matter of fact. As a goddess, the doings of the Sidhe had not been of much interest to her at the time, and when they had vanished, she had barely noticed. It really had not mattered much. It mattered now.

There *was* one person who could tell her what she wanted to know. The problem was she was terrified of him.

"Changelings" she read. "Often fairies would take a human child and replace it with a fairy child." Well, they had got that right at least, but nowhere did it say *why* the fairies were supposed to have done this although there were numerous speculations. Hecaté did not have to speculate, she knew why – Infiltration. And she realised, with a jolt, that this time it was happening on a wide scale – Stiles's missing baby cases. Denny had evidently worked this much out according to his notes on the subject. But he had not figured out all of it.

He had not seen the changeling right under his nose.

* * *

'Is he all right?'

'He's fine,' said Tamar impatiently, 'just knocked out.'

'Now what?' Denny did not waste time on recriminations, there was no point, Tamar would not have listened anyway.

'I'll wake him and we can ... can … get the hell out of *here* anyway. We need to talk.'

They limped, hobbled and dragged themselves back to the gypsy camp. None of them had ever been in such a bad way before; it was unnerving. Just a few hours in this cursed forest and they were wrecks of their former selves.

'But,' said Tamar, 'at least our minds are our own again.'

The gypsies scolded them for running off into the woods, particularly Denny whose injury was very bad they said.

Denny was mildly surprised – he had forgotten his wounded leg in all the excitement, and then he realised why. He looked down at his blood soaked trousers and saw that the blood had dried – there was no more leaking out. He stomped his leg on the ground, and there was no pain. His leg was sound.

'We *can* beat them,' he said. 'It was all in our minds. I *was* healed. You healed me just fine but I didn't believe it – they weren't letting me.'

'What has power like that?' mused Tamar.

'Actually, power over the mind isn't all that special,' said Denny. 'Hypnotists can do it and so on. The problem is that there's really no defence against it, unless you're prepared. We just didn't see it coming.'

'But we will now,' said Tamar fiercely.

'Mmm,' said Denny in a distracted fashion.

He turned to the gypsy king. 'Is there somewhere we can talk?' he asked. 'Alone.'

The gypsy king nodded and led them to his private tent and left them there.

'I don't trust them,' said Stiles unwarily as soon as the king was gone.

Tamar looked meaningfully at the tent flap, but Denny shook his head. 'It doesn't matter,' he said. 'If they *are* listening, then either we are not telling them anything they don't already know or they need to know this too. Either way it doesn't matter,' he reiterated.

Tamar argued with this. 'If they can't be trusted then surely we don't want them knowing how much *we* know,' she said.

'I guarantee, if they can't be trusted, it means they *already* know exactly how much we know,' said Denny. 'Besides, why shouldn't we trust them? They're only gypsies.'

'What exactly *do* we know?' asked Stiles, who did not think this was true, but knew there was no point in saying so.

'Not much,' admitted Denny.

'Tell us about the Sidhe,' said Tamar. 'How do I kill them?'

'Iron basically,' said Denny, smiling slightly at the way she put it. "How do *I* kill them?" 'As far as I know, it's the only way. Even this,' he withdrew the Athame, 'is no use against them.'

'No problem then,' said Tamar manifesting an iron bar.

'No good,' said Denny. 'It has to be *real* iron, manifestations are no good. Sorry.'

'Oh,' Tamar looked put out as she made the bar disappear or "unmanifested" it, as Cindy always said. She had said it so often that it had caught on among the others even though, as Denny pointed out, it was not a real word.

'You called them fairies,' put in Stiles.

'That's right,' said Denny. 'But don't be fooled, it makes them sound harmless, but they aren't. They're extremely dangerous.'

'We've noticed,' put in Tamar sourly.

'And ...' Denny looked at Stiles gravely, 'they steal children.'

He waited for the penny to drop. It did not take long.

'It was *them*?' Stiles snarled, going red with anger.

'You've heard of changelings?' Denny continued. Stiles nodded, unable to speak through his fury.

'If it helps, the children are probably all right.'

Stiles found his voice. 'Why?' he managed in a strangled tone.

'Nobody knows.' Denny sighed. 'What I *don't* understand is ... he broke off. 'Oh my God,' he gasped. 'I am so stupid. I can't believe I didn't see it before.'

'What?' said Tamar.

'*Changelings*,' said Denny. 'They usually grow up as a part of the family. No one ever suspects. *We* never suspected, even though he *is* such a little horror.'

'Jacky!' gasped Tamar and Stiles at the same time.

'I *said* he wasn't Eugene's kid,' added Tamar. 'I just never realised he wasn't Cindy's either.'

'We have to get back,' said Stiles. 'My wife is in the house with that ... *thing*!'

'But where's the *real* Jacky?' asked Tamar. 'And the rest of the missing kids for that matter?'

Denny shrugged. 'I don't have all the answers,' he said.

'But what do they *want*?' Tamar said plaintively. 'Why are they here?'

'Fun.' The voice was a soft female voice and it seemed to come from all around them. 'We want to have fun,'

* * *

Somehow, Hecaté realised, some of the parents were accidentally exposing the changeling in its true form. That was surely the only explanation for the mysterious transformations occurring. So why had it not happened here? And how many others were out there, that *had not* been exposed?

Many of the older children were, as Denny had surmised, acting – as she now recognised – like Faeries might be expected to. But it was only the very young – the babies – who had been exposed for what they were. Another clue? Were the older ones also changelings? Changelings who had not been exposed? How long had this been going on?

Long enough (and here she shuddered) for some of these to have grown to adulthood? She realised, with a shock, that Denny had thought so, and he was usually right about these things.

However, this was conjecture and more important to Hecaté, at the moment anyway, was the fact that once the changeling was exposed, the parents ceased to care for the interloper, and it ran away. She *had* to work out how to expose Jacky (or the thing that looked like Jacky) to Cindy. She decided to read Stiles's notes on the missing children, there might be a clue there, now that someone knew what they were looking for.

* * *

Three heads whipped round and saw her standing in a pool of scattered light. Tall, beautiful with a crown of pale green flowers atop her long golden hair. She was smiling. Silvery laughter filled the air around her.

'This was *our* world,' she said, 'long ago.'

'Until you were banished,' said Denny defiantly.

'We left,' she corrected him, but no one believed her. 'And now we are back.'

'You state the obvious beautifully,' sniped Tamar sarcastically.

Bright green eyes were turned on her with an expression that clearly said, "You are nothing. I could wipe you out without a second thought". They were not ordinary eyes. They were, when you looked into them, the cold dead eyes of a serial killer. Tamar stared back unflinchingly – no one else could have done it.

The Faerie gave in first. Tamar had a stare like a thermic lance and had probably been practising longer. It was the sort of thing she would do – gaze into a mirror until it broke out of sheer desperation.

As soon as she broke her gaze, Tamar grabbed Stiles and yelled at Denny. 'Now, go *now*!' and vanished.

Denny shrugged. He looked at the Faerie Queen.

'They will not get far,' she said.

'I wouldn't bet on that,' Denny told her. 'You don't know her like I do,'

'Why did *you* stay?' asked the Faerie Queen. 'I can no longer see your mind, it is like iron.

'I'm ready for you now,' he said.

The Queen nodded.

'I have questions,' said Denny.

'Ask.'

'You are Queen Onagh, the Queen of the Sidhe?' he began.

She nodded her assent, seemingly unsurprised at this evidence of her fame.

'The thing about a link between minds,' said Denny, apparently inconsequentially, 'is that it works both ways. Especially if the person whose mind you're trying to read has telepathic abilities of their own.' He looked slyly at her to see her reaction to this, almost certainly unexpected, development. Her face was carefully blank.

Satisfied, he continued. 'It *was* you in my head wasn't it?' he said. 'Don't bother ... I know,' he added before she could deny it. 'So I just have one question for you. What do you want with me?'

* * *

'Where's Denny?' Tamar panicked as they landed in a clearing, which was nowhere near where she had been aiming for, but one problem at a time. 'He should have been right behind us.'

'Maybe *he* went the *right* way,' groused Stiles from a pile of bracken, which was tearing his trousers as he tried to free himself.

Tamar glared. 'It doesn't work like that. He was following *me*. Or he should have been. So where *is* he?'

'When you put it like that,' Stiles admitted. 'It doesn't look good.

* * *

Denny was playing a dangerous game here, and he knew it. Keep her off balance long enough to get some answers, and still get away. But without answers, they did not stand a chance. He was not really surprised when he lost the game; he was playing with an empty deck.

Queen Onagh decided that she would not answer any more questions until she had him where she wanted him.

Resignedly, Denny had to let himself be captured by the enemy. It was the only way. He just had to make sure it was not *too* easy for her. As he half-heartedly ran away, he pondered on the last question he had asked her. He really wanted to know what she wanted him for. One thing he was certain of; he was not going to like it.

~ Chapter Seven ~

WHEN SHE FINALLY found it, Hecaté could hardly believe it. According to Stiles's notes, all the children were with someone at the time of their transmogrification. Well, she knew that. It tallied with her theory that the parents (or in some cases grandparents or even baby sitters) were the ones who had exposed the changeling, however unwittingly. But it was telling that it was not only parents who were able to do this. She was looking for general behaviour brought on by contact with young children. Something that anybody *might* do sometimes, but (and this was important) not all the time and not *every*body (*they* had not done it – obviously) and it had to be a recent development, something people did not do long ago, when the Faeries were here before. This ought to have narrowed the possibilities considerably, but she still had no idea what it could be.

Stiles's reports were thorough, but people could not be relied on for the details. She had briefly considered the telephone (another piece of modern technology that was utterly mysterious to her) the contact numbers of the parents were on the reports. But how exactly would she put it? – "I think your child may have been kidnapped by Faeries. What was the very last thing you did before your baby turned into a monster and flew away?" – people these days were far too clever to believe in such nonsense. Most of them believed that the government had been conducting genetic experiments. A few talked of aliens. None of them would believe in Faeries. Sometimes it was hard to make people believe the truth. It was usually too unbelievable.

So she turned back to Denny's notes. There turned out to be a chant in an old language, so old that even Hecaté could barely read, written as it was, in an ancient alphabet. It was supposed to reveal the changeling to human eyes. After several tries, she managed to sound it out and laughed all the way up the stairs to Cindy's room.

* * ,

Stiles was torn. On the one hand, Tamar was urging him to help her find Denny (who was probably in trouble (having been last seen in the company of the Faerie Queen) and going home to Hecaté who was *definitely* in trouble (being alone in the house with a known changeling who was also known to be extremely vicious). No one worried about Cindy since she seemed to be the only one that was not in any danger from Jacky.

In the end, it was decided that they should go after Denny since Tamar said that: A, she wasn't leaving without him, and B, her teleporting power seemed to be a bit off, and she could not guarantee *where* they would end up. Oh, and there was no chance of them making it home on foot since they were completely lost.

'If we don't stop the Sidhe,' she added. 'It won't matter anyway, because *no one* will be safe.' This was inarguable.

Stiles argued anyway (Tamar was rubbing off on him) but Tamar was better at it, and she won in the end.

'So,' said Stiles suddenly as they trudged through the trees. 'Was it real or not?'

This was unexpected and rather difficult.

Tamar rubbed her nose, a habit picked up from Denny, which meant that he was going to lie but was not happy about it. 'No,' she said.

'Ah,' said Stiles. 'No I thought not. I mean, we … you and I … I mean *us*! It's just not …'

'Exactly!' said Tamar. 'You love Hecaté and I love Denny, and we've had this conversation before anyway.'

Stiles was startled. It was true, but he had forgotten it until now. He nodded uncertainly but since he was behind Tamar, she did not see this.

She ploughed on. 'I mean, there might have been *something* there if it wasn't for the others, but it wouldn't have been real anyway. So just forget about it.'

'Yes,' agreed Stiles. Nevertheless, he continued to watch Tamar's backside as she walked ahead of him – but that is just men for you.

* * *

What do you want with me?' Denny was painfully aware that he was not in any position to be asking questions. He was chained up in dungeon. The chains and manacles appeared to have been wrought from some kind of bronze and the knife the Faerie Queen was wielding was perhaps made of stone – he was later to make the horrible discovery that the knife had actually been carved from a human femur.

She gave him a blank smile.

'I know you wanted me here, but I want to know wh…' Denny began.

She grasped his head and kissed him slowly.

It was all Denny could do to prevent himself from gagging.

'I think you know why,' she told him. 'But later, when you have been properly … indoctrinated

'Brainwashed you mean?' said Denny.

Not at all, you must open your mind, that is all. Perhaps I should have said, "Attuned". You must learn to understand us. To understand us *is* to love us.'

Denny seriously doubted this. He felt he already understood the Sidhe pretty well and love was the furthest thing from his mind.

'I have no intention of being banished again,' she said suddenly.

'Ah, so you *were* ...'

'I plan to stay this time.' She overrode him as if he had not spoken. 'The blood of a witch on the stones to bind us to the land and ...' She looked at Denny with a steely gaze. 'A human husband to bind me to its people.'

'*Husband*!' Denny almost shrieked. Obvious as it might be to you and me where this was going, he honestly had not seen it coming.

'I thought you already had a husband,' he added hopefully. He was sure he had read about this somewhere. Well, as sure as he could be about anything, circumstances being what they were.

'Oh ... him,' she said dismissively. And hope died.

'Why me?' he asked, truly perplexed.

'You have power,' she said. 'I sensed it the first time I entered your mind. 'And I don't mean this ...' she took the Athame from his belt, 'this borrowed power. I mean *real* power – power of the mind.'

Denny was disconcerted. He had not expected her to take the Athame, or even recognise it for what it was. He brought his mind back to the matter at hand and tried not to think about the sudden loss of his only advantage, or the fact that he was now a prisoner in actual fact rather than merely pretending to be one.

'I don't. I mean I don't know what you mean by that,' he tried.

'You are a natural leader of your people,' she said, and Denny nearly laughed out loud.

'You disagree?' she observed. 'But I know what I saw in your mind. You have saved the world several times. I read it there.'

'I didn't do it on my own,'

'You are the leader of these people,' she insisted, ignoring this disclaimer. 'They just are not aware of it. But where would they be without you? Dead – or worse, and I know about worse believe me. I can see to it that they understand all you have done for them. I can give you everything you ever wanted.'

'You have no idea what I want,'

'We can rule together,' she continued in what Denny now realised was a rehearsed monologue. 'All will worship us. These people, these pathetic sheep will be our slaves. It is the least that they owe you.'

'And that was the problem right there,' thought Denny. "Pathetic sheep". She had almost had him, he had to admit, until she said that. After all, a little appreciation would not have gone amiss. He had occasionally allowed admission to these thoughts, and she had clearly picked up on it.

But she had not understood him. He did not want to rule. He did not want to be worshipped. You could not treat people like that. If you did, then you stopped thinking of them as people. Of course, *she* did not think of them as people in the first place.

The needle on the record player of Denny's mind skidded suddenly backwards. 'What stones?' he asked.

Queen Onagh looked sharply at him. 'What?' she snapped.

'You said, "the blood of a witch on the stones to bind us to the land ...".' Then another thought struck him. 'What witch?'

The Queen smiled. 'I shall enjoy being married to you,' she said. 'I like a challenge.' She ruffled his hair. 'And you're cute too,'

Denny shivered. 'I *knew* I wasn't going to like it,' he thought.

'Yes but *what* witch?' he persisted. 'Too urgent,' he thought.

The Queen just laughed and snapped her fingers. Several Faeries appeared, as if from nowhere, with expressions on their beautiful faces that went far beyond ordinary malevolence. They surrounded him and regarded him with glowing eyes. Some of them giggled. They had a pent up excitement in their demeanour. And long sharp knives in their hands.

"Uh oh," thought Denny. Maybe being married was not the worst thing that could happen to him after all.

'It is time to begin your re-education,' she told him. 'When it is complete then you shall know everything.'

As she closed the door of the cell behind her, the Faeries swarmed at Denny.

At the sound of the first shriek, a smile flitted over her face. 'I do enjoy this part,' she murmured to herself.

* * *

Hecaté blew into Cindy's room and marched confidently to the terrible tot on the bed. Like Tamar before her, she swept the child up into her arms and held him up to the window in an iron grip. A look of alarm spread over the little features at this unanticipated show of spirit.

'Ahh,' began Hecaté carefully. 'Ooh a coochie coochie coo.'

* * *

'We're going in circles,' said Stiles

'How can you tell?' said Tamar. 'It all looks the same.'

'That's how I can tell.'

'Oh, well … you're probably right. Of course, it would help if we knew where we were supposed to be going.'

'You can't sense him at all?'

'Nothing, I can't even sense *you,* and you're right next to me. Something's interfering with my powers.'

'It's her.'

'I know – she's set her will against me. It's like blundering about in a fog.'

'So, where we want to go then, is wherever she doesn't want us to go, can you tell where that is?'

Tamar stopped and looked around her with her eyes closed – so to speak. Then she pointed. 'There!' she said. 'That's where we keep getting turned back.

'Sure?'

'Oh yes, it's like a strong wind blowing in my face now that I know what I'm looking for.'

'North,' said Stiles looking at his wrist.

'What's that?'

'Gadget that Hecaté got me for Christmas. Watch with a compass in it. Never thought I'd ever get to use the bloody thing, but it comes in handy now. I'm leading from now on,' he said firmly. 'I just keep going north, right? Just follow me.'

Tamar never wasted time arguing when something self-evidently made sense, and this did. Stiles's compass would not be subject to the strange forces that were interfering with her senses. He would follow that compass to the end of the world if necessary, and nothing would distract him. He was nothing if not dogged.

After only half an hour, they stopped because Stiles's compass suddenly flew out of his hand and stuck to a rock that was rearing straight up out of the ground as if it had been planted there.

Stiles cursed. 'Magnetic,' he said. 'We haven't been going north at all. The bloody needle was pointing at these.'

As they approached, they saw many more of the same type of large rocks arranged in a rough circle.

'What's a bloody Stonehenge doing in the middle of a wood, anyway?' said Stiles. 'What a waste of time.'

'No,' said Tamar. 'This is it all right. This is what she didn't want us to find. I wonder why?

'But what the hell are they?' she wondered wandering around the nearest one and feeling her jewellery tugging toward it.

'They are the Portal Stones,'

It needn't be said that this was not Stiles's voice.

Tamar knew without turning round that it was the gypsy king.

'What are they then?' she said trying to sound casual, although she felt as if she was on the brink of finding out something crucial.

'They guard the portal to the Faerie realm. They're there to keep them out – or in – however you want to look at it.'

'They failed then, didn't they?'

'They held her back for a thousand years,' he said defensively. 'I never thought she would get back again.'

There was something about the way he said this that made Stiles's radar twitch.

'You know her then?' he said on a hunch.

Tamar thought this was silly – how could he? But as it turned out, Stiles was right.

'Oh, I know her all right,' he said. 'I've known her for a thousand years.'

* * *

She was beautiful Denny supposed from a certain point of view. But, from another point of view, she was just – nothing. This was, Denny decided, because he was, in fact, seeing two of her at the same time. The real one and the one she wanted him to see. Had he been under her thrall, he would only have seen the beautiful image that she was projecting. As it was, it was confusing and a little nauseating.

The folk tales had said that the women of the Sidhe were hollow at the back; Denny was beginning to see what they meant. Onagh had no substance, only image. What you see from the front looks real, but from behind, you could see that there was nothing there. And Denny could – to coin a phrase – see right through her. It was hurting his eyes to look at her. His eyes kept straining to see what his brain was telling him was not there.

She would come in between torture sessions to gloat over him. She would stroke his bloodied and bruised face gently, almost lovingly, although Denny got the impression that it was the blood and pain she was fond of, rather than himself. She was never there when the torture was going on, although Denny had the idea that she had been watching. 'She probably has a special gallery,' he thought wryly.

Despite the fact that she was well aware that he was not under her control, she seemed to have no idea that he was not seeing her exactly as she wanted to be seen. It might be the reason that, although when she came to him, she was sweetly seductive, (no doubt the point of which was to show him the alternative to the torture he was undergoing – what he would have if he capitulated) she nevertheless seemed to pay scant attention to her attire. It was a supreme self-confidence that even Tamar could not equal. Even Tamar did not act as if she could get away with wearing just anything and still look good – even though she probably could.

This latest was interesting, Denny thought. She seemed to have picked up on the general idea but ...

'You do realise that negligee is on backwards?' he said.

* * *

The King bowed elegantly, disregarding their shocked expressions. 'Finvarra, High King of the Gypsies, Guardian of the Stones,' he said. 'Sorry about that, by the way,' he added. 'Can't think how she got past me.'

Stiles thought he knew how. Not the details, of course, but the general theory. Guarding something gets dull, especially after a thousand years and especially when you believe in your heart that what you are guarding is safe anyway. The Key Stones guarded the portal and Finvarra had relied on the stones. But *he* was supposed to guard the stones, and he had not.

Taking all this under consideration Stiles asked. 'Could someone open the portal from *this* side, get past the stones I mean?'

Finvarra had the grace to look embarrassed. 'But why would they?' he said.

'So they *could* then?' said Tamar pouncing on his uncertainty.

'Well, yes all *right*, I suppose so. But ...'

'One of yours?' asked Stiles.

'Oh, but ... they wouldn't. They *wouldn't*.' Finvarra insisted.

'No, probably not,' agreed Stiles. 'After all, if they were going to do it, why wait all this time?'

'What does she want with Denny?' asked Tamar abruptly.

'Denny?' Finvarra looked blank for a moment and then he said. 'You mean the other one, the blond haired one with the injury? She took him?'

'Yes.'

Finvarra shook his head. 'Oh dear, oh dear,' he said. 'She's at it again.'

'What?'

'She's going to marry him.'

'*Denny*?' spluttered Stiles in disbelief.

'But she's married already, isn't she?' said Tamar. 'I thought there was a king somewhere, isn't there?'

Finvarra shrugged as if this was irrelevant.

'*Denny*?' repeated Stiles. 'I mean, no offence to the guy, but why *him*? I don't get it.'

'I do,' said Tamar. 'After all, *I* want to marry him.'

'Yes but that's different. I mean why not pick a king or a president or something.'

'*I* didn't.'

'Yes but *she* could have picked *anyone* – someone with power and influence.'

Tamar cocked her head on one side. 'What's your point?' she asked.

'Ah, yes. I see what you mean.'

'How do we stop her?' asked Tamar, getting back to the point.

Finvarra looked puzzled. 'Stop her?'

'Ah!'

'Listen,' said Stiles, 'what I don't understand is why aren't you … I mean, why *weren't* you …? Oh, damn!'

'What we mean is, how are *you* involved in all this? How can you have known her for a thousand years? Aren't you human?' Tamar translated kindly.

'It's a long story,' said Finvarra. Then he caught sight of Tamar's expression. 'Suppose I tell you all about it?' he added hastily.

* * *

'Feeling any more amenable?'

Denny managed to raise his head with difficulty, and gave the Faerie Queen a sour look. 'Hardly,' he told her. 'You know torture isn't usually considered the best way to make friends and influence people.' He reconsidered this statement and added. 'Well make friends anyway.'

The Queen gave a silvery, tinkly laugh that made shivers run down Denny's spine. 'But what choice do I have?' she said.' Your mind is closed. It would have been so much easier the *other* way.'

'But not as much fun,' said Denny, astutely.

'I like talking to you,' she confided. 'We think alike.'

'I'm sorry you think so,' he told her. 'That was sarcasm in case you didn't realise.'

But Queen Onagh had not heard of sarcasm, so she chose to ignore this remark.

'My *last* husband wasn't like you at all,' she said.

'Is he dead?' asked Denny, slightly fearfully. He could easily imagine this creature killing a dozen husbands if she took it into her head.

'Dead? No,' she said. 'He's around somewhere. Hatching plots, I'll be bound. He betrayed me, you know.' She clenched her fists and bit her lips until the blood came. 'Betrayed *me* ... to *witches*!'

Denny closed his eyes. 'Tell me more,' he thought fervently. 'Tell me *everything*.'

* * *

'Let's get one thing straight,' said Finvarra. 'I'm not on your side or anything. I mean I'm not human after all. Not exactly, I just rule them. '

'The gypsies?' asked Stiles.

Finvarra nodded. 'For several generations now. They are the natural enemies of the Sidhe,' he added. 'It seemed a good choice.'

'So then, you're not exactly on *her* side either?' said Tamar.'

'If it came right down to it ... no I suppose not. We've been estranged for a long time.' He sighed. 'She always gets it wrong,' he said obscurely. 'No patience. The time is not yet.' He seemed to be talking to himself. Tamar noted his words carefully – she would work out what they meant later. For example, what did he mean *estranged*?

'Tell us about the Key Stones,' she said.

'Witches put up the stones to guard the portal after she went through.' Finvarra told them. 'She wasn't exactly banished you see, just prevented from coming back through. In those days, before the stones were raised, the door was always open, and they came through whenever they wanted, but their court was in the Faerie realm. But she went too far you see, she wanted to rule, tried to marry the King, had him right under her thumb. They do that you see. Folk see them the way they want them to. Except witches and druids – they see everything the way it really is. Anyway, it was a reign of terror. People locked their doors and hid under the bed with a handy piece of iron. Horseshoes nailed to the door, that kind of thing. Happy days,' he smiled reminiscently.

Tamar gave him a look. He coughed self-consciously

'Ahem! Anyway a bunch of witches decided enough was enough, so they raised the stones one Winter Solstice night when most of the Sidhe were feasting at court.'

'But not all of them?'

Finvarra looked surprised. 'No there *were* some stragglers,' he admitted. 'How did you know that?'

Tamar shrugged. 'Call it a hunch,' she said looking hard at Finvarra. He did not flinch.

'The witches knew they wouldn't live forever,' he continued, 'so they made a deal with me to guard the stones.'

'Why did you agree?' asked Stiles.

A cunning look crept over the king's face. 'It was me or her,' he said. 'Besides, it's been so peaceful without her.'

'What do you mean, it was you or her?' said Stiles. 'Did the witches threaten you?'

'No,' said Tamar. 'That's not what he meant.'

'He's not telling us everything,' she thought, 'not by a long shot. – Like who the hell he really is'.

'I should get after your friend before it's too late,' said Finvarra, abruptly cutting off this line of speculation

She's set up Court over there,' he pointed approximately east according to the setting sun (Stiles's compass was now merely decoration) 'about five leagues as the buzzard flies. I should get a move on if I were you.'

Tamar merely stared at him until he began to shift uncomfortably.

'Well, I'll just get out of your way …' he began.

'How do we send her back?' said Stiles baldly.

'You can't.' said Finvarra. 'You'll have to kill her.'

'Okay,' said Tamar calmly. 'How do we do that?'

'You can't expect me to tell you that,' objected Finvarra. What am I, an idiot?'

'What kills her, kills you too?' said Tamar. She was fishing here, but she was almost certain she was right.

'I never said that.'

'But it's obvious,' put in Stiles. Who had no idea where she was going with this but was backing her up valiantly anyway.

'Iron,' added Tamar in a very low voice.

Finvarra gave in. 'Oh, all *right*,' he said. 'I suppose it's better than being dead. But if you want to send her back, you'll have to do it before she binds herself to the land.'

'Spill it,' commanded Tamar. '*All* of it.'

* * *

Witches always see things exactly as they are.

Of course, they do not always necessarily understand *what* they are seeing. This was particularly true of Cindy, who had always been a bit blonde.

When Hecaté had performed the chant and exposed the changeling, Cindy's reaction had been a disappointing 'So what?'

Even Jacky had looked surprised, but only for a moment, then he had merely looked smug.

Clearly, Cindy had been seeing the changeling as he was all along, but it had apparently never occurred to her that he was not her son.

Of all the possible outcomes of her plan, Hecaté had not even considered that it would make absolutely no difference at all.

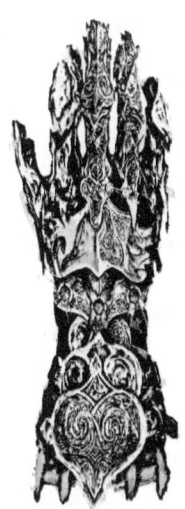

~ Chapter Eight ~

TAMAR LET STILES handle the interrogation. Well, each to his strengths. She handled the glowering menacingly and the filtering of Finvarra's lies into an approximation of the truth.

When she thought that they had extracted as much from him as they were going to Tamar reached inside her jacket and pulled from somewhere (probably another dimension) a long iron sword and cut his head off. Before the head had even rolled, the whole body had turned into a gelatinous goo. They watched it seep into the grass.

'One down,' she said. 'Let's go get the rest.'

'Why did you do that?'

'He'd have been as bad as her,' said Tamar. 'He's one of *them*. What do you think he's been doing here all these years, painting the flowers, mending shoes? What do you think he meant by "it's not time yet"? He wanted what *she* wants. He set himself up as a king over the gypsies didn't he? They can't help themselves. But he wanted her out of the way first, and he was waiting for something else too.'

'What?

'We'll never know now, and it doesn't matter anymore.'

'But you could have just sent him back.'

'No! No more Faeries, if *she* got back through, he might have too – one day. We have to get rid of them all – like … like wasps.'

'So why did you make him tell us about the stones?'

'Ha! To see if he would. He was scared. Scared because we knew about the iron. That's all I wanted to know.'

'That's nasty.'

'It's going to get nastier.

'Where did you get that sword anyway? I thought Denny said manifestations wouldn't work.'

'I didn't manifest it. I called for it. Denny's got a whole collection of this stuff, in the attic. He doesn't use it anymore, since he got the Athame.'

'You *called* for it? I never heard of that before'

Tamar looked smug. 'Very tough magic that,' she said, 'especially when you don't know where you are. That's why I usually manifest stuff. It's much easier.'

Another thought struck Stiles. 'A whole collection?' he asked.

Tamar grinned. 'Yeah.'

'Can *I* have one then?'

'Only if you promise to be careful.'

Stiles gave this some thought. 'I'll be careful to kill every Faerie that I see,' he promised.

'All right then.'

'So,' said Stiles, 'let's go and find the nest.'

* * *

'*She* is coming here.'

'Who?'

'The raven haired one, the one with the bad temper.'

Denny said nothing.

'Well?' she snapped.

'What?'

'She is coming for *you*?'

'So I imagine.'

'Why?'

'She saw me first.'

* * *

'But he *isn't* your child,' Hecaté had Cindy by the shoulders and was shaking her.

'Whose is he then?' asked Cindy perplexed.

'He's a changeling, you know a Faerie child – *look* at him.'

Cindy looked. 'He looks like my uncle Ray,' she said.

'For Hades' sake Cindy, he's got *wings*!'*

'Apart from that of course.'

'And you did not wonder about that?'

'Well, what with Eugene being an angel and everything I just ... I don't know. Are you *sure* about this?'

'How do you not fall on your face more?' asked Hecaté in exasperation.

'What?'

'Anyway the few Nephilim that do have wings, have *angelic* wings, not Faerie wings like those. Do those look like *angel's* wings to you? And they do not get them until adulthood anyway.'

The what?'

'The children of women and angels – the Nephilim. You did not think you were the first did you?'

'I never thought about it,'

'Very well,' said Hecaté. 'Watch this.' And she waved an iron skillet that she had taken the precaution of hiding amongst her clothes. Jacky shrank visibly.

'See?' she said. 'He's afraid of the iron.'

Maternal instinct took over. 'Don't you hurt him,' shouted Cindy, grabbing Jacky and holding him to her body protectively.

'He's *not* Jacky!' yelled Hecaté coming incautiously towards them still holding the skillet. But Cindy had had enough. She dumped Jacky behind her on the bed, grabbed an extremely heavy glass bedside lamp and swung.

---

* Traditionally the Sidhe do not have wings of the body any more than humans do. But all Faerie children are born with wings, which drop off about age three. No one knows why this should be

As Hecaté lay on the bedroom floor, unmoving, Jacky came and took Cindy's hand, he grinned malevolently. 'Come on Mummy,' he said. 'It's time.'

Cindy looked blankly at him. 'All right dear,' she said.

If you go down to the woods today, you're in for a big surprise.

~ Chapter Nine ~

IT WAS A PALACE – that was what Stiles could not quite believe. An actual goddamned for-real fairy palace – with turrets. Tamar was not a bit surprised.

It stood on a hill that certainly had not been there before, in fact, it seemed to float just above and in front of the landscape, a bit like a very realistic hologram. Tamar thought it had been grafted on to the scenery rather than fitted into it, and if you looked properly at it, it appeared that the rest of the terrain had been subtly moved out of the way to make room for it. For some reason, this made her intensely angry.

Stiles just stared at it in wonder.

'Weapons?' she snapped to bring Stiles back to the matter at hand.

'Check,' said Stiles automatically.

'Good, you guard the gate,' she said unexpectedly. 'I'm going in alone.'

'Oh no you bloody well are *not*!'

Tamar gave him the benefit of her best steely-eyed gaze, which impressed him not at all.

'Do you really want to argue with me right now?' she said dryly

'Yes.'

'This is between me and her,' said Tamar.

'Yes,' agreed Stiles. 'But a bit of back-up never hurt. Anyway, I'm coming, so get used to it.'

Tamar opened her mouth to argue but Stiles forestalled her. 'He's my *friend* Tamar.' he said gently.

Tamar just stared at Stiles with her mouth open as if she had not even considered this.

She gulped guiltily once or twice. 'Right,' she managed. 'Come on then.'

'They'll be expecting us,' Tamar cautioned Stiles.

'I know,'

'But I've got an idea,'

The doors stood open with only two door wards guarding it. Tamar tornadoed* into the castle — a lithe chain mail clad figure wielding the biggest sword this side of the Middle Ages. Knocking Faeries to the left and right of her – those of them, anyway, who were incautious enough to get near to her. The rest she ignored. Stiles could mop them up.

Stiles was finding his chain mail a little cumbersome, but he was glad of it anyway. The Faeries clearly had not expected it, and they shied away from it as if it burned. He was sweating and short of breath in the heavy helmet and breastplate; in fact, he was certain that he was going to have a heart attack, and he was as happy as he had ever been in his life.

Tamar seemed to be enjoying herself too. This was what life was all about. Swinging a great heavy sword while the Faeries ran and screamed.

* * *

Denny knew he was dying. He just did not know exactly how long it was going to take. He had never been tortured to death before.

---

* Like storming in, but more so. Tamar did not have a motto, but if she had, it would have been along the lines of "Enough is never enough" or even "*Too much* is never enough" or possibly "If a thing's worth doing, it's worth overdoing"

She knew it of course, and she would save him if he capitulated. But it was too high a price to pay. The old Denny would have scoffed at this idea, being a pragmatist of the first order. How could there be too high a price for your *life*? But now he understood. She had given him a glimpse into her world – the world inside her head – and it was empty, like her. A mere glamour, no substance. No human could live like that. It would be like being dead with the unfortunate drawback that you would be alive to suffer it.

Of course, he would escape if he possibly could, that was different. But she had taken the Athame – it was standing in a lump of rock not more than a few feet from him. A particularly ingenious bit of cruelty in which she had taken immense delight. He could see it but not reach it and, frankly, even if he could have, he was not sure he would have the strength to remove it now anyway. Of course, the Athame itself would give him the strength, but he was not able to realise that now. He could barely think straight.

His mind was slipping; he was finding it increasingly difficult to think about anything but the pain.

'Iron,' he thought vaguely. 'Iron to bind.' Well he had no iron, but something was nagging at him something else in the same context but different. 'Iron to bind ... and ... and ...'

Iron was how you killed Faeries, but he could not kill them. Even if he had had iron he was in no condition to ... it was something else ... not to kill. Something that you would not think of as a weapon. Not to kill but ... they were afraid of iron, and they liked ... something they liked? That did not make sense. Denny was aware that he was becoming incoherent – Faeries tend to have this effect. He tried to focus his mind. 'Iron to bind and ...'

His train of thought was interrupted by a crash. He heard screaming. Despite his agony, he grinned. Tamar.

Of course, it was too late for him, he could not last much longer and anyway *she* would have him killed rather than let Tamar have him. But Tamar would not have thought of that. She always went at everything like a mad bull at a gate.

Consequences were something that happened to other people in Tamar's private universe.

Still, he would be avenged at least. Tamar would never let it go. She never let anything go.

She came in. 'I'll see you dead first,' she told him.

Denny nodded.

She turned to a contingent of faeries that had followed her in. 'Kill him,' she ordered. 'Quickly,' she added. 'No fun, just do it and then meet us at the stones.

'At least we can do *that*,' she muttered to herself.

She turned to Denny. 'I wanted it to be *you*,' she said. 'But I *will* find another. Fool, I could have given you *everything* and your rejection will not change the outcome.'

And she swept out of the room.

'Blah blah blah!' thought Denny.

'Make it quick boys,' he said as the Faeries closed in. 'You heard the lady.' He closed his eyes and an explosion took place in his cerebrum. Of *course*, he had had a weapon against the Sidhe all along. Only he had not seen it as a weapon. Because Faeries loved it, loved it so much that it made them dippy. 'Iron to bind and *music* to maze.'

He hummed a few experimental opening bars.

The effect was electric. The Faeries were fascinated. They stopped and stared at him with their mouths open. He charged up the beat and began to sing. And Denny could really sing. The Faeries began to dance. He felt like the pied piper.

* * *

'What's that?' said Tamar as they ran down a deserted corridor.

Stiles listened. 'Sounds like "Come on Eileen".'

Tamar smiled. 'Denny.'

'But why would he be singing?'

'*I* don't know, maybe it's a signal, maybe he heard us coming. Where's it coming from?'

Stiles looked around wildly, as if that would help, and noticed something else.

'Where the hell is everyone?'

'Sshhh!'

Tamar lifted her head and closed her eyes to listen. It is incredibly difficult to isolate the direction of a distant sound – it always sounds as if it's coming from everywhere.

Then she looked down suddenly. 'It's coming from underneath us,' she said.

'Dungeons?' said Stiles.

Tamar rolled her eyes. 'I might have known,' she said disparagingly.

* * *

The problem with this plan, Denny was realising, was that he could not keep it up forever. His voice was beginning to crack although the dancing Faeries did not seem to have noticed (it does not have to be fantastic music. Faeries are fascinated by *any* music).

He had been weak to begin with, and now he felt exhausted. He hoped to God that Tamar found him soon.

* * *

As Tamar burst into the dungeon, the already befuddled Faeries scattered in disarray. Tamar never noticed them go – she was staring in horror at Denny. 'Oh *no!*' she gasped.

Flayed and flambéed, he was chained to a pillar and looked as if he might be already dead.

However, he must have been semi-conscious because he flinched away with a look of terror that wrenched at Tamar's heart when she raised the sword to cut his bonds.

'*No!*' he screamed. Then, his legs folded up beneath him and he collapsed to the floor like a puppet that has had its strings cut.

He looked up ruefully at her from the floor. 'They broke my bloody legs,' he told her wryly.

Tamar gathered him up. 'How did they do this to you?'

Denny pointed to the Athame sticking up out of the rock. Tamar nodded. At that moment, Stiles arrived and took in the scene.

Tamar turned to him.

'There's about a hundred of them upstairs,' he said.'

Tamar's face was grim. She lifted Denny and reached out her hand towards the Athame, which flew, into her hand.

She nodded to Stiles. 'Burn it down,' she said callously.

Stiles looked at the wreck of Denny, his expression grim 'Right!' he said curtly.

Tamar disappeared with Denny in her arms.

* * *

The Athame could not heal, its only defect – a remnant of its history as a demonic weapon. Tamar could heal though, but it was going slowly. Denny had lost consciousness again after Tamar healed his broken legs. This had hurt a lot. Magical healing is not a case of waving your hands about and praying (that's faith healing). Magical healing works like regular healing only a lot faster. And Tamar was crying a lot.

She had thought that she had hated Askphrit, but she realised now that that hatred had been a pale thing compared to her hatred of the Queen of the Sidhe. What was 5000 years of servitude compared to *this*?

She shuddered. *Don't think about that.* Denny had saved her from that, and that was that.

And if she lost Denny …

It was a distinct possibility. It was too soon to tell, but they might have got to him too late. Even with her accelerated healing powers, there comes a point of no return for everybody. Not even Tamar could raise the dead. And Denny was failing fast.

His skin was healing, and he was beginning to look more like himself. He opened his eyes, and Tamar felt her heart beat faster. He tried to speak.

'Shh,' she told him. 'It's okay, wait until you're stronger.'

He shook his head frantically. 'No,' he said. 'You have to find the Queen. She's going to kill Cindy.'

Behind them, the flames rose from the Faerie palace.

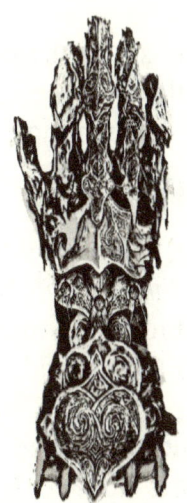

~ Chapter Ten ~

'WHERE?' DEMANDED TAMAR.

'I dunno. She mentioned st-stones. That was it – the blood of the witch on the stones. I – I don't know where ...'

'*I* do.'

Denny smiled. 'Of course you do,' he said.

'How is he?' Stiles knelt down beside the prostrate Denny. 'Oh Jesus!' he said.

'No, he's past the worst now,' said Tamar. 'Take care of him.' And before Stiles could argue, she rose to her feet and took off to the stones.

'What the hell...?' began Stiles. But Denny had passed out again.

This time Tamar knew exactly where she was going, she could feel the pull of the stones from here. It took her a few moments to realise that this was because she was wearing a hundred pounds of iron chain mail and not due to any mystical senses that she might possess. It came in handy though.

She could see the fire through the trees. Hundreds of shadowy figures shimmered darkly against the flames. There was laughter and muffled screams. And from the centre of the circle, only just discernible against the background of smoke from the fire, a fog was rising.

Tamar felt frozen to the spot – helpless. She could not see Cindy, although she could hear her. Then, even that was drowned out by the sound of chanting. Low at first, so low that she could not make out the words, then louder and louder, faster and faster escalating to frenzy.

'*Kill the witch, spill her blood, seal the spell.*'

'*Kill the witch, cut her throat, spill her blood.*'

Still Tamar could not move. Horror had taken hold of her and her legs felt rooted to the ground, spellbound by a morbid fascination.

The Faeries were dancing around the fire like savages at some horrible cannibalistic feast. It gave Tamar an idea. Unfortunately, her legs still felt like they were stuck in concrete.

The chanting stopped abruptly, and the spell broke over Tamar like a crashing wave. She staggered in the immensity of the sudden, heavy silence that fell and a hideous dread came over her.

The Faeries gathered.

A pulsing beat came thumping through the trees. The Faeries turned in helpless fascination as Tamar came strolling towards the fire with a massive ghetto blaster perched on her shoulder.

* * *

Denny opened his eyes and sat up suddenly. 'Where's the Athame?' he croaked.

Stiles was amused despite himself. 'Feeling better?' he asked. He handed Denny the Athame, still stuck in its bit of rock.

'Tamar couldn't get it out,' said Stiles. 'But I think she was pretty confident that you would be able to.'

Denny pulled it. It slid out easily, and Denny grinned.

'It belongs to you,' said Stiles solemnly.

Denny laughed. 'The old sword in the stone trick?' he said. 'Nah, this is Tamar's idea of a pick me up. She was just trying to boost me up or something.' He waved the stone at Stiles. 'It's not even the same rock.'

Stiles deflated. 'Oh,'

Denny shifted himself upright. 'Gone has she?' he asked.

'Yeah. You know where?'

'Let's get after her then,' said Denny. 'Before she does something – you know – Tamar-like. I'll explain on the way. You'll have to lead, though.'

'I will?'

Denny looked concerned suddenly. 'You *do* know the way to the stones, don't you?' he asked. 'I mean I just assumed ...'

'Why has she gone *there*?'

Denny looked relieved. 'Come on,' he said. 'Like I said, I'll explain on the way.'

Denny did not put his authoritarian head on very often, but when he did – it was strange Stiles thought – but whole armies would have followed him. Stiles had no chance.

'All right,' he said.

* * *

Tamar pushed her way through the dancing Faeries, ignoring them, until she reached Cindy who was tied to a stake in the middle of the stones and looking terrified. Tamar marched up to her and cut her bonds with the sword. Cindy identified her then. 'Oh, Tamar,' she gasped. 'I knew you'd come. You or Denny at least, but probably you. Where is Denny? – And Jack,' she added as an afterthought.'

Tamar turned cold eyes on Cindy. 'Run,' she said.

'I didn't mean to hurt her,' babbled Cindy. I mean I didn't know what I was doing, but she'll be all right, I mean she's a *goddess*. Oh, and they took my boy.' The words ended on a sob.'

Tamar softened a little. 'I know,' she said. 'I'm sorry.'

'But you can get him back for me.' It was not a question, it was a statement made with absolute certainty.

Tamar hesitated. Then she took Cindy by the shoulders. 'I'll do my best,' she promised. 'Now you have to get out of here. Denny and Jack are in the woods somewhere. Okay?'

Cindy nodded, satisfied. If Tamar said she would do her best, then it was as good as done. Tamar *never* failed.

When she had gone, Tamar turned to the Faerie Queen, who was swaying slightly with a blank look on her face, and slapped her across the face.

The Queen passed from semi-comatose to completely alert (and angry) in less than a split second.

'This is *my* world!' Tamar told her. 'Get Out!'

* * *

By a fortunate coincidence Cindy ran almost straight into Denny (a not altogether unpleasant experience, but she was too distraught to appreciate it) and Stiles.

'Where's Tamar?' snapped Denny looking over her head urgently.

'B-back there,' stammered Cindy pointing behind her.

Denny almost threw Cindy at Stiles and carried on running.

Stiles faltered and stopped short hanging on to Cindy, he watched helplessly as Denny disappeared into the shadows 'I guess it's all up to them now,' he said.

* * *

Hecaté came round slowly to find the changeling pulling on her arm.

'Wake up, wake up,' it snarled angrily.

Hecaté went from horizontal to vertical in one smooth, horrified movement. 'Urrrgh,' she exclaimed involuntarily.

'No time, no time,' wailed the changeling. 'Must help. *She's* got her.'

Hecaté made no answer to this extraordinary statement, of which she could make neither head nor tail. Instead, she turned away with extreme dignity and walked haughtily away fighting down the instinct to run.

But the changeling was not giving up so easily. It flew in front of her blocking the doorway. 'Please,' it begged plaintively.

Hecaté stopped short. This behaviour was sufficiently uncharacteristic to get her attention.

'Suppose you explain what you are talking about,' she said cautiously. 'I am not saying that I will believe you, however,' she added.

'She took Mummy,' said the changeling. 'She took her for bad things, and the king is't there, and I don' know what t' do.'

It occurred to Hecaté that the changeling did not just *look* like a child – it *was* a child, albeit a Faerie child. She wondered how she was to make sense of whatever it was trying, apparently quite desperately, to tell her.

She decided to start at the beginning. *Who* has taken your … Cindy?' she asked.

* * *

'Jacky was taking me to someone called Finvarra,' said Cindy breathlessly as they ran along. 'Then *she* came out of nowhere, and about a hundred Faeries grabbed me and … and … can we stop a minute please?'

Stiles skidded to a halt. '*Who* came out of nowhere, the Queen?' he asked.

'That's what they called her,' agreed Cindy.

'What happened to Ja … the changeling?'

'He kind of freaked out. I don't know what happened to him after that. They were too many for him. He's only little.'

'So,' said Stiles slowly trying to get a handle on this unexpected development. 'He – it wasn't with *her*?'

'No, definitely not,' said Cindy positively. 'He tried to save me from her. But he couldn't.'

'Oh,' said Stiles. 'That's a twist.'

~ Chapter Eleven ~

'THIS IS *my* world – Get out!'

The Faerie Queen smiled and shrugged at Tamar. 'Very well then,' she said and stepped lightly to one side and vanished between the stones.

Tamar gaped. It *couldn't* be that easy. There *had* to be a catch.

'There is,' said Denny reading her mind. 'She expects you to go after her. – But you aren't that stupid of course,' he added artfully. Knowing full well that that was precisely what the vengeful Tamar wanted to do.

'I'm not? I mean – I am?' said Tamar bewildered.

'*She* has the power in there.' Denny said. 'Stands to reason, it's *her* world. And you can't take any iron with you through those stones because of the magnetism.'

'I know,' said Tamar. 'But if we just leave her there, she'll come back,' she added.

'Well?' Denny waited.

'I know what you're thinking, but I *can't* seal up the portal,' said Tamar. 'It takes the blood of a witch. A *lot* of blood.' She shuddered. 'That's what she was trying to do with Cindy. She was going to seal herself on *this* side of the portal.'

'Oh,' said Denny. 'How do you know all this?'

'A little Faerie told me,'

'Have you been "questioning" people again?'

'No, Jack did the questioning. I just looked scary.'

'Then I suppose the information is bona fide,' Denny conceded. No one could resist Tamar's icy glare. Even vampires crumbled – even gods. 'So what do we do?'

Tamar shrugged. 'We wait I guess,' she said, ''till she comes back. It doesn't matter anyway. I'm going to have to face her sooner or later. And better on my turf than hers.'

Denny nodded. 'That's sense,' he said.

'After all,' she added wickedly. 'I'm certainly not stupid enough to go after her.'

'Of course you aren't.'

'I mean, that's just what she *wants*, isn't it?'

'All right, all right, you've made your point.'

Tamar smiled, softly serious. 'Thank you Denny.

'Anyway,' she continued briskly. 'In the meantime, we have more than enough to do here.'

They looked around them at the still maniacally dancing Faeries. Tamar hefted her sword.

'Let's start with this lot then,'

* * *

'Jacky said that this Finvarra wanted to see me, that I would be safe there. He didn't explain it very well, but he must have meant from – you know… *her*!'

'Queen Onagh,' muttered Stiles. Then he turned sternly to Cindy. 'That … *creature* isn't Jacky you know.'

Cindy dropped her eyes. I know,' she said quietly. 'But I don't know what else to call him.'

'It,' corrected Stiles.

Cindy shuddered. 'Don't!' she begged. 'I mean, I fed him, bathed him, sang him to sleep. I can't think about … not now.'

Stiles relented. 'Not now then,' he agreed.

'Perhaps we should find this Finvarra,' suggested Cindy after a short silence.

'That'll be awkward,' said Stiles. 'He's dead.'

* * *

Hecaté had slowly pieced together, from the changeling's ramblings, the following facts. (Always assuming it was telling the truth, and Hecaté was not taking anything on faith)

One: that the changeling was not a part of the Faerie Queen's court, and he had been born in *this* world.

Two: he had been placed with Cindy by King Finvarra (whoever *he* was) to watch over her when the King had discovered that the Faerie Queen had returned. He did not know how the king knew that the Queen would go after Cindy, but somehow he did. Cindy's real baby was safe with King Finvarra; only the king knew where he was.

Three: having been brought up by Cindy for the last two years, he thought of her as his real mother and was desperately unhappy that the Queen had got her.

Four: the Queen was going to kill Cindy.

Five: King Finvarra was going to be furious when he found out.

Six: Denny was also in unspecified danger from the Queen. That was why he had bitten his leg, to keep him from going back into the forest. But it had not worked. And now everyone had gone, and it was all Tamar's fault – he did not like Tamar, she was hard like iron. (Hecaté thought this was a little unfair although she could see what he meant)

Having got all this sorted out, Hecaté decided that she had no choice but to go herself with the changeling (who, if he was telling the truth, she decided, she and the others had seriously misunderstood) into the forest.

Hecaté was not afraid of Faeries, having indeed, a store of supernatural powers of her own, not, in fact, dissimilar in origin to that which the Faeries themselves wielded. Of course, she was not as powerful as Tamar, but she felt that, should she need to, she could hold her own.

She found that she was actually looking forward to it. It had been too long since she had been in a good fight. Besides, Cindy was her subject. It was her responsibility to protect and guide witches. Cindy was also her friend. Whichever way you looked at it, there was no getting out of it.

She concentrated, reaching out with her mind until she located Cindy's aura (it was pink and fluffy with just a hint of mauve from the worry). Then it was just a case of moving herself into it. It's a god thing.

So, narrative flow being what it is – she just so happened to arrive in Cindy's wake at that same moment that Stiles was telling her that Finvarra was dead.

Quick as thought, Hecaté grabbed the changeling before he could fly at Stiles in fury.

It wailed in horrible, gut wrenching sorrow.

Cindy and Stiles whipped round stunned at the terrible sound and Cindy had to grab Stiles before he could fly at the changeling.

Then suddenly all hostilities were interrupted. The air turned cold and a strong wind bore down through the forest, sweeping the trees over like a windswept cornfield and sucking the breath from them like a vacuum. Then there was a loud boom and silence.

'Uh oh,' said the changeling.

'What?' asked Hecaté, who felt she now had some sort of rapport with the changeling. 'What is it?'

'It's comin' back,' announced the changeling. 'Duck!'

* * *

'What the hell was that?' said Denny picking himself up.

Tamar was shaking whether with fury or fear was yet to be determined, but probably the former knowing Tamar.

'That?' she said. 'That wasn't anything. That was just to get our attention.'

'Well,' said Denny. 'It got mine all right. It felt like the world just turned inside out.'

'Sod it,' said Tamar suddenly. 'I'm going home.'

'What, why?'

'Because *they* want me to stay here.'

* * *

'It came from the stones,' said Stiles. 'That direction,' he pointed.

Witches always see things the way they are. This is because natural intuition in witches is honed so sharply, as part of their training, that it almost seems like a second sight.

Cindy had a premonition. 'If we go to the stones,' she said, reading Stiles's thoughts, 'it will be bad.'

Hecaté looked sharply at her. She really was a more accomplished witch than she let on at times.

Stiles looked questioningly at Hecaté, more out of custom than anything else. She nodded. 'My sister is correct,' she said. Cindy glowed.

Stiles shrugged. 'Okay then,' he said. 'God knows, it's all right with me.'

'But where are Tamar and Denny?' asked Hecaté.

'We don't know,' said Stiles. 'They went to the stones but ...'

'Don' like T'mar,' put in the changeling.

Cindy took him from Hecaté and held him up to her face. 'If it wasn't for Tamar,' she told him. 'I would be dead right now. She saved my life.'

The changeling pouted but said no more.

'Tamar and Denny are at home,' said Hecaté suddenly.

It's a god thing.

~ Chapter Twelve ~

IT WAS NOT so much an argument as a very loud seven sided discussion – with added misunderstandings. Seven sided instead of five because several people, most notably Hecaté and Cindy, were changing sides at the drop of a pointy hat; and all this was accompanied by the incessant wailing of the changeling.

It was Denny who had thought to ask him what his real name was. This was two hours into the discussion, and it really had not helped matters when the changeling had given him a bemused look and said 'Jacky Pittencherry.' This had set Tamar off again and begun another three cornered argument between her, Cindy and Hecaté, who were respectively against, for and neutral on the subject.

It was never clear what began the argument in the first place – they were all on the same side surely? But none of them ever forgot what ended it.

In a rare lull in the shouting, Tamar thought she heard a knocking at the door. Denny thought it was more like a desperate hammering.

They both flew to the door; Tamar won naturally and flung it open triumphantly only to be trampled down by a crowd of frantic people from the local village.

They had come to escape the Faeries.

This was the only place they could think of that might be safe. There had been rumours about "the house" ever since it had turned up (while of course having always been there). People said that it was a good place to come if you were in trouble. And they were *all* in trouble now.

Some people had gone away to the city, but they wouldn't be any safer there, the people said darkly. Tamar was inclined to agree. There were lots of people still in the village, they said, locked in their homes too afraid even to come out.

Tamar decided to go and have a look. Denny said he would go with her. In the end, they all decided to go.

* * *

The village was dark. Every window was unlit every door fastened shut. There was a heavy silence, not even a dog barked.

On almost every locked door was a horseshoe. Many front steps sported a saucer of milk.

'Legends,' said Hecaté. 'People remember through the ages, even long after the true facts are forgotten. Nail some iron to the door or plant a rowan tree to keep out the Faeries, a saucer of milk, ha! As if that can appease them. As if they were cats. Even cats are not that cruel.'

'But it's rather like that, isn't it?' said Denny. 'Cats play with their victims – like Faeries. Don't you think a mouse would put out a saucer of milk for a cat if it could?'

'And it wouldn't do any more good than it's doing here,' Hecaté told him. Faeries take the milk and then they still want their fun!'

'Like cats.'

To Tamar, all these things told a different story. 'This has been going on for a while,' she said. 'This kind of terror doesn't happen overnight.'

She slammed her fist into her palm. 'We were being distracted!' she said angrily. 'All that business in the forest. It was to keep us away from *this*! I don't know why they bothered.'

She turned on the changeling. 'And what did *you* know about all this?' she snarled.

'Nothin',' he asserted. 'I's for the king,'

'He's telling the truth,' said Cindy defensively.

Tamar glared at the changeling for a minute; then she relaxed. 'He is isn't he?' she said. It was the first time she had said "he" and not "it"

Suddenly, it had seemed as if the changeling had come into focus before her eyes. She saw nothing but a lost, frightened child among hostile strangers. No wonder he had been so bad tempered and suspicious. So what if he was a Faerie? It's not what you are, but how you live that is important, and Jacky had been raised by Cindy who, though she could be vain and a little dim and was often inappropriately flirtatious, yet had a stern set of values, particularly pertaining to the misuse of magical powers. Not many children have such an example. Most parents do not have magical powers to misuse.

'It's worse than we thought,' said Stiles appearing round a corner. He sighed. It was, it seemed, his lot in life to be the one who found the corpses.

There were not many – two or three. One hanging from a tree, it was difficult to know whether he had been murdered or driven to suicide.

'It all comes to the same thing,' said Tamar.

'So, where are the Faeries?' said Cindy, for once putting her finger on the nub of the matter.

'In the woods,' said Denny. 'But they'll be back.'

'Soon, I think,' said Stiles looking around at the deserted streets. 'I reckon it's only like this when they're expected.'

'Oh they're expected all right,' said Tamar the light of battle in her eyes.

She concentrated, and four suits of armour and three swords clattered on to the ground in front of them.

'Suit up everyone,' she said.

'Where did these come from?' asked Cindy.

'Best if you don't ask,' said Stiles. 'What you don't know you can't tell the police.'

'Oh.'

Denny was amused to observe that his suit had a label on the inside that read "property of the ------ Metropolitan Museum".

A distant chattering sound and the sound of muffled laugher heralded the arrival of the Faeries.

Well they would not be laughing long, Tamar thought, scraping her sword along the ground like the hooves of an impatient bull.

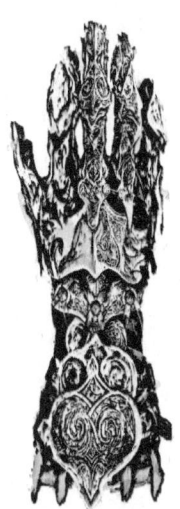

~ Chapter Thirteen ~

TAMAR WAS GAZING despondently out of the bedroom window. The battle in the village had been but the first of many such skirmishes and the problem was now spreading like wildfire up and down the country. They went out every night, the house was now full of refugees, they had taught people about the iron and how to fight back, and it was not even making a dent.

The situation was far worse than they had imagined. There were Faeries *everywhere*!

As if a signal had been given, thousands of changelings had apparently shed their incognito, and many of them were fully adult. How long had this been going on right under their noses?

It had clearly been the return of the Queen that had set recent events in motion. Like a catalyst, her mere presence had drawn them out. Not until she had come back and set up her court, had the changelings begun showing the true evil of their natures. Until then, no one had suspected a thing.

And then there were the Faeries who had come through the portal with the Queen. What they had seen in the castle had apparently been only the minutest fraction of the whole. Clearly, Queen Onagh meant business; she appeared to have emptied the entire Faerie realm.

And where was *she* now?

'I should never have let her escape' thought Tamar. 'If I'd known what she was up to, I wouldn't have.'

Tamar was out of her depth, and she knew it. She was not used to an arch villain with a long-term plan and the patience to put it into action. Ambitions yes! They all had those. Crazy plans for world domination, usually based on some insane premise, that was certain to fail in the face of a bit of determined opposition.

Now she really *did* miss Askphrit. At least with him, it had been *personal*. He had hated her, and it had clouded his judgement. World domination had always been a secondary consideration with him. And he had been reassuringly selfish. You could always rely on him to make some predictable move if he thought his own skin might be in jeopardy.

The Faerie Queen did not even have a decent maniacal laugh.

Denny came into the room and sat down silently. He knew something of how she was feeling. He waited.

'I'm losing,' she said. She would not look at him. 'There's just too *many* of them. I've never seen anything like this before. I mean what do they all *want*?'

Still Denny said nothing.

'We tried to teach people to fight back but it's not *working*! The Faeries just tell them not to and they don't. How do you fight magic like that? – I don't know what to do, there's nothing I *can* do.' She bit her knuckles in frustration.

Denny put an arm around her shoulder. 'Maybe,' he said. 'There might be something *we* can do.'

She stared at him guiltily.

'You don't have to take it all on yourself, you know,' he said. 'We're all fighting this one.'

'I know, and I'm sorry, I didn't mean it that way. It's just … well … *we're* losing Denny.'

'You'll think of something,' he said. 'You always do.'

'We've beaten Djinn, vampires, gods, even the rotten little clerks in mainframe, and *they* run the whole universe,' she said. 'I can't believe we've met our Waterloo with a bunch of *Faeries* of all things.'

This was bad.

'First of all, we aren't beaten yet,' admonished Denny. 'And furthermore, they may be *called* "Faeries", but they have more in common with the old style gods than storybook pixies. And there are thousands of them too. So don't beat yourself up on that account. We may have never faced such an enemy before.'

'You don't give a lot of pep talks do you?'

'I never had to before.'

'*We* need help, Denny,' she wailed. '*We* can't do this by *our*selves and if people can't even be taught to help *themselves* … it'd be a help anyway,' she finished off, muttering.

Denny knew what she meant. It was too much to expect them to fight *all* the Faeries by themselves, but that was just what they were having to do. *Try* to do, he corrected himself.

He took her face in his hands. 'We'll beat them Tam … *No* one can beat you, I really believe that. I've seen you do some amazing things, you'll think of something.'

'I just hope I think of something before the world ends,' she said gloomily.

'Sorry,' she added seeing his face fall.

She brightened up slightly. 'Maybe *you'll* think of something,' she said. 'It wouldn't be the first time.'

He smiled. 'Maybe I will.'

She snuggled closer to him. 'Denny,' she whispered softly in his ear.

'Yes?'

'Talking of doing something amazing …'

'Yes?'

'Lock the door.'

Denny raised an eyebrow. 'Now?'

'Now!'

Denny locked the door. Well, they did have a lot of house guests at the moment.

* * *

There had been no sign of the King's gypsies. This could be considered unfortunate since they might have made reasonable allies. Not allies they could trust of course, but at least allies that hated the Queen as much as they did and had definitely got some defence against the Faerie magic, probably learned from Finvarra himself. This would have been a big help.

It was a damn shame then that they all seemed to have vanished. Stiles opinion was that they were all dead by now or defected to the enemy. He had heard Finvarra himself say that, after all, he was not human when all was said and done. And, besides, they were still the number one suspects, in Stiles's opinion, for the opening of the portal. Stiles still thought they were probably Faeries too, or at least allied to them. Finvarra definitely was – or had been. Hadn't Hecaté said there were *only* bad Faeries?

Tamar was of the opinion that they were still out there somewhere, biding their time.

'Biding their time until what?' said Stiles sceptically.

'We don't know is the point,' she said and glared at him until he changed the subject. Tamar hated admitting that she did not know absolutely everything there was to know.

'Well, we couldn't have trusted them anyway,' said Stiles diplomatically. 'This is *our* fight.'

'It's like a war out there,' said Cindy.

'It *is* a war out there,' said Denny gently correcting her. 'I heard some of the old folks talking,' he continued. 'They were saying that it's worse than the blitz.'

There was a silence at this.

'B-but old people don't think that *anything* is worse than the blitz,' stammered Tamar. 'I've heard them, even the apocalypse war wasn't as bad as the blitz, I mean according to them.'

'Wasn't an apocalypse,' said Stiles. 'I mean we're all still here, aren't we?'

'Not for much longer if this carries on,' said Tamar.

'Worse than the apocalypse,' muttered Denny. 'Sounds about right to me.'

Hecaté, who had been listening in silence with Jacky on her knee, now stood up suddenly, accidentally depositing her burden headfirst onto the rug.

'Well,' she said, so much for our gallant heroes, if you could only hear yourselves. I suppose you are just going to give up are you?'

'Of course we aren't!' said Tamar. 'No one said we were giving up it's just … I mean they're everywhere now. Thousands of them and no one else seems to be able to fight them. There just aren't enough of us.'

'We'd need a small army,' put in Denny.

Tamar raised her head sharply at this; her eyes grew wide for a moment and then she seemed to be thinking deeply.

Only Denny noticed this. 'She's having an idea,' he thought. 'It's about bloody time.'

'A small army?' she said. 'I might know where I can get one of those.'

Everyone looked at her.

'They're fearsome fighters,' she added, 'especially with a drink or two inside them. They hate Faeries and each one comes with his own armour and weapons. A great saving.'

'Who are …?' began Stiles.

'And they aren't affected by Faerie magic at all,' she finished triumphantly.

'They sound perfect,' said Stiles. 'Who are we talking about?'

'Dwarfs,' said Denny. 'She's talking about Dwarfs. But we can't have any because they all buggered off to Valhalla – I wish *I* had.'

'I reckon I know how to find them,' said Tamar.

'Oh, no,' said Denny. 'We *promised*. No more messing about in mainframe.'

'It's an emergency,' said Tamar stubbornly.

'Anyway, what makes you think they'll agree?' said Denny. 'They might not want to fight, and they don't exactly like you, you know.'

'Not want to *fight*?' laughed Tamar. '*Dwarfs* not want to fight? You aren't serious.'

He's got a point though,' said Stiles. 'They might not do it if *you* ask. Just to be awkward.'

Tamar grinned like a happy cat. 'That's why I'm taking you,' she said. 'They like *you*.'

'Ooh, a *small* army,' chirruped Cindy suddenly. 'I get it.'

~ Chapter Fourteen ~

GETTING INTO MAINFRAME these days was a bit like riding a bike, as the saying goes. Denny could even get them directly into the file that they wanted. Of course, the clerks had changed all the passwords after the last time – just because they had promised not to do it again, did not mean that the clerks trusted them.

Denny had got the new passwords in his spare time – not to use them of course (he had *promised*) but just out of idle curiosity.

Tamar was amused when Denny reluctantly admitted that he could get them into Valhalla as soon as they liked.

'Well,' she had mocked. 'It seems that your integrity won't stand up to much scrutiny after all.'

'Shut up!' said Denny, but mildly, 'or I'll send you to Milton Keynes.'

'Do they have Dwarfs there?' asked Cindy innocently.

Denny looked sharply at her. Sometimes he felt her dumb blonde routine was a bit over-acted really. He knew damn well that she was not *that* stupid.

'No, he said flatly, 'just gnomes.' He heard Cindy smother a laugh.

Their eyes met, and Denny shook his head reprovingly, but he was smiling. 'Have it your own way,' she read in his eyes. 'But I know better.'

He tapped at the computer. 'Sure you want to do this?' he asked, bringing up the file.

'Yes,'

'No.'

Tamar looked at Stiles in surprise. 'I thought you liked Dwarfs?' she said.

''Tisn't the Dwarfs,' he muttered.

'Viking's're okay,' said Denny, who had once met some and got on famously with them.

S'not that either,'

'Look,' said Tamar, who exercised her very own brand of morality, 'it isn't breaking the rules if *we're* doing it.'

Stiles looked dubious about this.

'And you don't have to have a drink if you'd rather not,' added Cindy brightly, demonstrating a degree of insight that Tamar, at least, would not have thought she had in her. She was apparently right anyway. Stiles looked unaccountably relieved at this summation.

'You won't be there that long anyway,' she added.

'That's right,' said Tamar. 'Just in – get the dwarfs – out again.'

Denny slid out of the chair. 'Anyone not going to Valhalla stand back from the computer.' he said.

Tamar stepped forward with Stiles and pressed, "Enter". 'All aboard,' she said, and they vanished.

* * *

'Are you sure this is the right place?'

'Looks right,' said Tamar. 'See, large mountain over there, large mountain over there, absolutely bloody enormous mountain over there.'

'I see,' said Stiles dryly. 'But there are, as far as I can see, and not to put too fine a point on it, no Vikings – or Dwarfs either,' he added.

'They're all inside getting drunk,' said Tamar authoritatively.

'Inside where?'

'Um,' said Tamar, scanning the skyline.

'Anyway, I thought they battled all day and drank all night.'

'Pure hearsay,' said a voice from behind them. A deep, booming voice that could only belong to a man with more testosterone in him than a football team locker room.

Tamar's spine prickled. She turned round cautiously. 'Hog?' she gasped.

'Djinn,' said the Viking pleasantly. If he was surprised to see her, he was hiding it well.

'We don't fight *every* day,' he went on as if nothing at all surprising had happened at all. 'We aren't barbarians you know. At least, not anymore.' He said this rather sadly.

Stiles stares at him. Taking in the large hairy chest, the huge untamed beard, the goatskin jerkin and the horned helmet.

'Really?' he said.

'Oh no, we've evolved, so they tell me. I don't know, fifteen hundred years dead, and suddenly we find out that we've been doing it all wrong. It's a sad day when a proud warrior meets his descendants and finds out that they make furniture. I mean what kind of a job is that for a race of conquerors?'

'So, you two know each other then?' said Stiles in a frantic effort to change the subject. It was embarrassing watching fifteen stone of hairy Viking with tears dripping down his nose.

'Jack, this is Hogswill the Hairy Backed,' said Tamar wearily. 'We used to hang out – well I was in a bottle most of the time but it was still quite an education. 'Hog, this is Jack – stop blubbering will you – he's a po-lice-man. That means he asks difficult questions and always knows when you are lying. Where are the dwarfs?'

'In the tavern of course,' said Hogswill, blinking rapidly in his nervousness. In his experience, only the Norns knew when a man was lying, and they were women. He eyed Stiles apprehensively as if expecting him to suddenly don a corset and start singing in a high falsetto voice. (Something *actual* women never do, but Hogswill was getting confused)

'Of course they are,' said Tamar. 'Can you take us to them please?'

'*Please*?' thought Stiles.

Hogswill also seemed a little thrown off by Tamar's good manners. Even as his slave, he remembered, she had tended to treat him with barely veiled contempt.

'Well ...' began Hogswill nervously. 'There are no women allowed see. 'Cept serving wenches o' course.'

'I'm not a woman,' snapped Tamar, 'I'm a Djinn. That's different.'

'Oh, is it?' said Hogswill the not overly bright. 'I suppose that's all right then.'

'What do you want with dwarfs then?' he ventured as they trotted along.

'We only want to borrow them for a while,' said Tamar. 'We need some fighting done.'

'Fighting,' said Hogswill dreamily. 'They're good you know,' he added. 'Fearsome little buggers, very handy with an axe.'

'Yes, I know.'

'Who are you fighting then?' he asked.

'Faeries,' said Stiles, before he could stop himself, and immediately regretted it. He expected this giant to laugh heartily at this, but he did not. Instead, he stopped short in the road with his mouth hanging open and turned an interesting shade of putty.

He worked his mouth a few times without saying anything then he leaned down to Tamar and whispered hoarsely. 'Älvor?'

Tamar nodded briskly. 'That's right,' she said.

Hogswill gulped a few times to calm himself down.

'Come back have they?' he said eventually.

'With a vengeance,' said Stiles.

'Ah, they always come with vengeance,' said Hogswill knowingly. 'Little bastards.' He added with feeling. 'Do they still steal babbies?'

'Yes,' said Tamar shortly.

'Little bastards,' repeated Hogswill.

'You know,' he added thoughtfully. 'Me and the lads might like to help out too. I mean we've a bit of a score to settle if you know what I mean?'

'You can't,' said Tamar flatly. 'You're human and you know what the – er – Älvor do to humans. We'll just take the dwarfs thank you, as many as you can spare.'

Hogswill took off his helmet slowly and scratched his head.

'I reckon …' he said after a few minutes thought. 'I reckon it ain't so – exactly.'

'What isn't?' said Tamar impatiently.

'I mean ter say,' he said ponderously, 'I meantersay, we ain't human anymore. I mean we was, but now we ain't, if you see what I mean.' He beamed, happy to have managed his delivery of this radical bit of metaphysical thought.

He thought some more. 'I reckon it's like this. When we're here, we're human, right? But if we was to go back, we'd be like ghosts. The living can't hurt ghosts'

'Hmm,' said Tamar.

'Anyway I reckon some of the lads ud like to try,' he added hopefully.

'Well okay, you ask them then,' said Tamar. She leaned over to Stiles and whispered. 'It can't hurt to try,'

'Here we are then,' boomed Hogswill, suddenly.

* * *

The tavern did not look any better from the inside than it had from the outside, and from the outside it had looked like a shack.

'Little brothers are in the far corner,' said Hogswill helpfully pointing to a gloomy, shadow filled rats nest at the back of the tavern.

'Thank you,' said Tamar stiffly. 'You go and ask them,' she said to Stiles, 'I'd better keep out of the way.' But it was too late.

'Snow White S'welp me,' came a voice from the region of her knees, but it was said without rancour, apparently as a matter of form. It was Florid.

Florid Underdrawers the King of the Dwarfs bowed ironically to Tamar; so low that his nose was touching the floor.

'And what can we do for you *this* time?' he asked acerbically. 'World need saving again?'

'Yes,' said Stiles, thinking he had better take a hand.

'Jack Stiles?' said the Dwarf delightedly. 'Is that you?'

Stiles knelt down. 'Hello Florid,' he said. 'How's the afterlife treating you?'

Tamar sighed. Jack had a rapport with the Dwarfs that was entirely beyond her comprehension. To her, they were smelly, bad tempered drunken little buggers. To him, they were *compadrés*, buddies, just some of the lads – only smaller and with a much larger drinking capacity.

Florid was herding Stiles enthusiastically towards the other Dwarfs, leaving Tamar standing alone and feeling terribly exposed. She was drawing curious looks from the drinkers to which she reacted with her famous thousand kilowatt stare. Stiles looked back anxiously at her, but she smiled reassuringly at him. The mission was all that mattered.

She heard the shouts of greeting from the dwarf table, and above the ruckus she heard Stiles say. 'What's everybody drinking then?'

It was that sort of thing, she thought, that made him popular. He seemed to know, instinctively, just the right thing to say. Good old Jack, everybody's best mate. Even she liked him, and, apart from Denny, she hardly liked anybody.

A Viking came up behind her and said something muffled in which she could just make out the words "comely wench"

'Oh, no!' she thought. 'I'm not being "comely wenched" by anyone.'

This was, after all, only the dark ages by default. She moved slightly and somehow the Viking ended up on the floor bubbling in agony. Tamar folded her arms and pursed her lips in a pose universally recognized by men as "I'm not in the mood". Several formerly interested Vikings averted their eyes and shuffled round in their chairs back to their drinks.

There was a chorus of exclamations from the corner and then a muffled argument started.

'He's told them,' she thought. 'Now they'll argue about it for two hours until Florid tells them they've got to do it.'

She was painfully familiar with the Dwarf version of democracy. Florid was only supposed to be nominally in charge; that is, he ruled with the helpful suggestions of at least thirty Dwarfs, all with opposing opinions, and then he told them what they had to do, and they did it. Which made him *actually* in charge, in Tamar's book. But Dwarfs like to have their say, it made them feel better apparently. It was a democratically run dictatorship.

This time it was different. Tamar was surprised when Florid presented himself to her after only ten minutes, bowed (this time without a trace of irony) and said. 'We will help,'

And that, apparently, was that. Within twenty minutes Florid had gathered an impressive army of five hundred grim faced Dwarfs.

'They hardly argued about it at all,' Stiles told her. 'And when Florid pointed out that even if they died, they could still come back here, it was pretty much settled.'

'He didn't have to order them or *anything*?'

'Oh I think he *would* have, but he didn't have to. They really *hate* Faeries.'

'Doesn't everybody?'

'Not like this.' said Stiles somberly. 'This is something different.'

'Good,' said Tamar. 'Then I made the right call.'

A tentative hand tapped Tamar on the shoulder. She turned round.

'Er, are you the Djinn?' said a rather fresh faced youth with bulging muscles that would have made Cindy swoon, and a worried expression.

'That's me,' said Tamar wondering what on earth he wanted. He did not seem the "comely wench" type. For one thing, she was sure he would not even know what to do with a comely wench if he had one.

'Only we were wondering where you wanted the army,' he said.

'You were saying,' said Stiles.

Tamar recovered fast. 'Fall in with the dwarfs,' she said. 'Shoulder to shoulder – everyone must be touching. 'I'll handle the transportation.

'Will they all fit in the living room?' said Stiles.

'They'd better,' said Tamar. 'EVERYBODY READY?' she bellowed. 'Close file.'

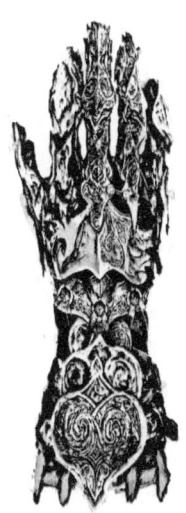

~ Chapter Fifteen ~

DENNY WAS SITTING stretched out in an armchair; eyes half closed, pondering things. So he was not very pleased to be interrupted, but as it was a young woman who looked extremely nervous, he forced himself to be courteous.

'I was just wondering …' she began.

'Yes?'

'Um …'

She twisted her hands around each other, and her eyes swivelled nervously around the room.

'Well?' he said as kindly as possible.

'Do you think I'm pretty?'

Oh no, not this *again,* 'CINDY!'

Cindy hurried into the room. Denny wearily indicated the young woman who was gazing at Denny with embarrassing adoration.

'She's been "Faeried",' he said. 'Sort her out will you? Thanks.'

Cindy bustled the young woman unwillingly from the room. 'You'll thank me later,' she told her. 'Besides he's attached and you don't want to mess with *her*, believe me!'

It had happened to all of them in the past few weeks. In fact, it seemed to be happening all over the house. But it was happening to Denny an awful lot. Women all over the house seemed to be making a beeline for him. He had occasionally wondered what it was like to be a chick magnet. As it turned out, it was horribly unsettling. Denny had no illusions about himself; women tended to look past him to see if he had a better-looking friend. He suspected the Queen was behind it, but he could not think of a single reason, sheer malice apart, why she would be doing this to him.

It was not just the lovey dovey stuff of course. They were also dealing with random fights every day and people who believed they could fly or that they were a rabbit or something. It was like running a rehab centre, with electro shock therapy as a mandatory treatment.[*]

Just when it seemed to be settling down, a fresh influx of people would arrive, and it seemed that they brought the Faeries enchantment in with them – like a virus – and it would start all over again.

And every day more people turned up. Word had got around; it was safe here, at least safer than anywhere else. At least the Faeries themselves could not get in. It occurred to Denny that the Faeries were sending people here who were enchanted, just to disrupt things. The sensible thing would be to just close the doors for good, but how could they turn them away when they had nowhere else to go? Another problem was that they were running out of space. Soon it would be standing room only.

Very soon, in fact.

It was very lucky for Denny really that when five hundred heavily armed dwarfs and two thousand, three hundred and seventy seven Viking warriors landed in his living room that he was not actually there. Only a few minutes earlier and he would most definitely have been human sushi.

---

[*] It had been discovered, after much experimentation and several instances of second-degree burns, that an actual bolt of lighting was not necessary to lift the Faerie enchantment. A fairly mild electric shock would do the trick

They did just about fit, mainly because dwarfs are ... well, dwarf sized, and the Viking warriors, as Hogswill had predicted, turned up as ghosts, and ghosts do not take up any room at all in a physical sense. But it was still a tight squeeze and frankly, in their current surroundings, they made a fearsome sight.

Tamar acted fast. Before they even had time to catch their breath she managed to teleport all the dwarfs into the grounds. The Vikings, as spirits, could not be moved in this way since teleportation relies on the astral plane and they were already there in a manner of speaking (although they were on the physical plane as well, at least visually) and they just had to drift through the walls after them as best they could.

Denny, who was in the garden at the time got a front row view of possibly the weirdest sight he had ever seen; and that, in his case, was really saying something.

First, he saw the aforementioned five hundred dwarfs appear suddenly on the lawn, in the flowerbeds, in the pond and one in a tree. They were all bickering loudly and waving their axes menacingly. ''Ere, give us some room.' 'Watch what you're doin' with that axe,' etc.

As incredible as this sight was, it was nothing to what came next, as spectral Viking warriors began drifting slowly through the walls in ones and twos, until all the available space between the Dwarfs was filled.

'Bloody hell!' said Denny, impressed. 'An army of the dead.'

* * *

Once Tamar got going, generally speaking, there was no stopping her. The last time she had built an army she had made it from golems – any three dimensional image of a human being with life breathed into it magically can be a golem – and she had made the golems from anything and everything she could think of. Scarecrows, shop dummies, even cigar store Indians had been pressed into service alongside the more conventional statues and terracotta warriors.

Now she was talking excitedly about enlarging this army. 'Trolls,' she said. 'Trolls are pretty vicious and too stupid to be enthralled by Faerie magic. You need to *have* a mind before it can be controlled.'

'No trolls,' said Denny patiently. 'Too dangerous to the general population.'

'Gnomes?'

'Too small to be any use,' said Denny firmly. 'Besides, aren't they just a form of Faerie? Could we really trust them?'

'Well. Witches then,' she tried. 'Witches aren't susceptible to Faerie magic.'

Denny guardedly conceded that actually witches might not be a bad idea. 'They were the ones who sorted the Faeries out the last time weren't they?' he said thoughtfully.

Tamar, as was her wont, took this qualified and cautious agreement as a full acquiescence to her whole plan. Trolls, gnomes and anything else that came to mind included.

She was smart enough not to tell Denny this, however. This time she didn't want talking out of it.

* * *

The ghostly warriors proved to have an unexpected and highly gratifying effect on the Faeries that Tamar tried them out on. Everyone had been wondering exactly what use a ghost would be at fighting, since they tended to go right through things at the drop of a horned thing that you wear on your head. So Tamar decided on a trial run, and the results were incredible.

The Faeries, one and all, fainted dead away. Not at the *sight* of the ghosts (Faeries deal out fear they do not suffer from it). The mere presence of a spirit seemed to make any Faeries within a certain radius just pass out even if they had not seen it.

The only problem was that the moment a ghost made a Faerie faint it also disappeared. Presumably, and it was certainly hoped anyway, back to Valhalla.

No one knew why it was happening although Denny theorised that it was because the ghosts were on another plane of existence and the Faeries were *from* another plane of existence, neither of which was real in *this* plane of existence, and they were effectively cancelling each other out when their auras came too close. No one knew if he was right about this and it all sounded very complicated and mystical. But it *was* true that none of the Faeries affected in this way ever woke up again. It was as if their spirit had been drained away leaving only an empty shell. Killing them would have been kinder. But Tamar was not interested in being kind to Faeries. Besides, enough of them *would* die.

They had no idea what was about to hit them.

* * *

Tamar surveyed her army with satisfaction. They were pretty frightening although Denny had voiced the opinion that what they really needed was the *Salvation* Army.

'Big brass band,' he had explained to the blank faces turned to him.

'Right,' said Tamar, never one to dismiss a good idea when it was handed to her on a platter. 'We need a marching song then.' She looked at Denny sideways. 'That should help, shouldn't it?'

'Enormously I would have thought,' he said.

They had been unable to add any witches to the ranks. For some reason, there were none to be found even when Tamar cheated and asked Hecaté to use her powers to find some.

However, in addition to the Dwarfs, Vikings, Trolls (only indistinguishable from the Vikings by their size – the Vikings were slightly larger) and Gnomes, they also had battalions of Minotaur, Centaur, Satyr, Faun, and Unicorns, all of whom Tamar had rounded up from Hank's Mythological Wildlife Preserve in the hidden forest just behind the swing park near Denny's old flat.

Tamar had them all lined up in a large field behind the house. It looked like the casting session for a rather overambitious fantasy movie.

What all these creatures had in common (in common with each other and with human beings) was that they had all suffered at the hands of the Faeries.

Payback's a bitch.

'And so am I,' thought Tamar.

It would be a glorious battle.

What a pity she would not be there to see it.

~ Chapter Sixteen ~

TAMAR SPLIT THE army into four divisions and put Denny, Stiles, Hogswill and Florid in charge of the various divisions. She was a natural born General. The divisions were necessary to split up those species who naturally did not get on together. She did not want the Dwarfs (who had trouble with metaphor anyway) to take the phrase "bury the hatchet" to a literal extreme. Which, had they been forced to fight alongside the trolls, might be a real hazard. Centaurs and Minotaurs also had to be kept apart although the reasons for this were now long buried in the past and possibly the only person present (Centaur and Minotaur included) who remembered them was Tamar herself.

The Vikings (who were technically human and did not annoy anybody – except Tamar) were split up between divisions.

It was assumed that Tamar would be taking charge of the army. So when she told Denny that she wanted him to do it, as well as looking after his own division (Trolls, Vikings and Unicorns – the most unruly of the warriors you may notice) he was stunned.

'B-but it's *your* army,' he stuttered. 'Don't *you* want to ...?'

It was time to tell him the truth; there was no more room for evasion.

'I won't be there,' she told him bluntly. 'I have something else I have to do. And if you ask me what it is, I'm going to lie to you, so don't.'

Denny knew Tamar well enough to know that this was true. And that she was not leaving on the eve of battle, as it were, out of fear. On the contrary, she was probably leaving to do something even more dangerous. If he knew what it was he would probably only worry, so he did not push it.

* * *

In a few hours, it would be nightfall, time to move out. Tamar was on the veranda with Stiles.

'We could all die you know,' said Stiles gloomily. His own division (Centaurs, Satyrs, Vikings and Gnomes) were bickering endlessly and refused to take direction – he would rather have had the Dwarfs, but, much as they liked him, they would only follow Florid in battle.

'It's the chance we take,' said Tamar.

Stiles nodded gloomily. 'It's the waiting that gets me,' he said. 'I don't mind the fighting so much.'

'You'll be leaving soon I suppose,' he added.

Stiles had been informed of Tamar's imminent departure by a bewildered Denny and had decided that it was none of his business. But old habits die hard so he asked anyway.

'When you do,' she said. 'In a few hours.'

'It's the waiting that's hard,' repeated Stiles. 'Seems a long time to kill until sundown.'

'Don't waste it then,' said Tamar.

'What are *you* going to do for the next five hours then?'

'Say goodbye to Denny,' she said. 'That should take a good few hours to do properly. Go and say goodbye to Hecaté. I should.'

* * *

'Denny?'

Denny turned in surprise. 'Oh, I thought you might have gone already,' he said.

'Not yet,' she said. 'Soon, but I wanted to say goodbye.'

She stood awkwardly in the doorway.

'Goodbye?' said Denny. Then a light dawned. 'Oh, *goodbye*. Right.'

He locked the door.

* * *

Denny was up. He stared out of the window at the falling dusk. In a few hours they were all going to die, he knew it his heart, there was no way out of this one. It was a hopeless fight, but they were going to do it anyway.

'We should have got married,' he said suddenly.

Tamar sat up sharply. 'What?' she said.

'Yeah,' he continued. 'It wasn't that I didn't *want* to. You know that, right? It was just ...'

'It was always going to be something,' supplied Tamar. *Why did he have to start this now?*

'That's not a good reason,' he said. 'I realise that now. I mean, if it's always going to be *something*, then we should have just done it anyway. I'm sorry.'

'Don't be,' she said. 'It was me too.'

'Yeah,' he agreed. 'But if I'd have ...'

'Forget it,' she said. *It's too late now anyway.*

* * *

Tamar watched the troops file away with a sense of terrible hopelessness. Whatever they achieved would only be a small victory, and they would pay dearly for it. But it was better than nothing. Better to die fighting than live under the enchantment of the Faeries. Better to try than to give up. But this time, there would be no last minute intervention, no sudden twist that would turn hopeless defeat into victory. No tricks this time, she was out of tricks. And she had battle of her own to fight.

As the last of her army disappeared into the night, she turned and headed for the basement.

Basements in any large house are interesting places. Full of gloomy, mysterious corners and odd shaped dustsheets, hidden doorways often leading to the wine cellar or occasionally outdoors onto a small patio. The hidden doorways in this cellar led to much more interesting places than that. Just about anywhere you could think of actually. This was due to the fact that the whole house was only nominally on this plane of existence and below the house was access to the mainframe central offices. Clive, the clerk who had previously owned the house had used it to get to work. From there one could also access all the files from mainframe, if you knew how to do it of course. It was still stuck on the hall of images, the file that Clive had last opened before he had left the house to Tamar and Denny. No one, not even Denny, had been able to figure out how it worked.

The hall of images was actually a repository for the image of any being that's existence was focus of belief (gods for example). People need an image of something to believe in it, and this was where the images were stored. They looked like statues. Many of them had been destroyed.

Tamar walked past the dusty images and the broken statues, some no more than a pile of dust, until she found the one she wanted. Funny that none of the others had noticed it. Yet it made sense in a strange sort of way. She was a mythological creature generated by belief although not by anyone else's belief in her, just her own belief in herself, which had been unshakable for 5000 years. Until now.

Now the image was showing cracks and soon, if she did not do something, it would crumble like all the others.

Probably the only thing holding it together at all was Denny's continued belief in her. And that would die with him, she thought grimly.

Under the pedestal was a small door. She opened it. Inside was a dusty, grimy bottle, which she gingerly removed.

She stared at it unwillingly for a long time then she closed her eyes and concentrated.

And vanished inside the bottle.

* * *

The Faeries had been expecting them, but of course, this was anticipated. The army had, in fact, simply marched out in the full expectation of being ambushed.[*]

Denny raised his sword above his head as Faeries swarmed them from all sides.

'All right lads,' he yelled. 'Let's get 'em.'

A forest of swords appeared raised in the air. The Faeries whooped and attacked.

All else was drowned in the sound of clashing steel.

---

[*] Allowing your troops to be ambushed is, in fact, a standard military manoeuvre, just not one that any army in the world will admit to (presumably, because it does not sound very tough). It gives you the advantage, however, of not having to bother to go and find your enemy and choosing the battleground yourself.

Part 2

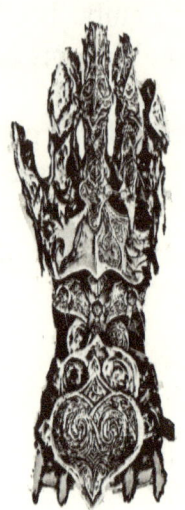

~ Chapter Seventeen ~

Six weeks later...

THERE WERE BODIES everywhere. The streets were littered with the remains of Tamar's army, left just as they fell among the rubble of now deserted streets. A macabre and careless graveyard over which lay a ghostly white fog as if to soften its grisliness. But no one ever went there now to see it.

Almost no one ...

The white robed figure who drifted among the slain did so with a sense of purpose, as if she knew exactly who she was looking for.

She found Denny first. He was lying in a twisted position, his head flung back awkwardly, his legs awry, a gaping wound in his side, there was no doubt that he was dead. The sword he had carried was still gripped tightly in his hand. He looked strangely uncorrupted for a six week old corpse. He might have only just died that night.

The figure bent over his body reverently, touched him lightly and passed on.

Next, she found Jack Stiles, and here she hesitated. His body was in a much worse condition, badly wounded in many places and it appeared that his neck was broken – the head does not usually sit at a 90° angle to the neck. But he also appeared very recently deceased. A pathologist would have been extremely confused. The robed figure bent down and touched him lightly and this time waited for a few moments before passing on.

Then Cindy, who had somehow managed to achieve the neatest death ever seen. Not that she was not badly wounded – she was. It was just that she did not have a hair out of place and she was lying on her back with her arms folded as if she were already in the casket. Even her lipstick had not been smudged. There was something fundamentally unshakable about Cindy's pride in her appearance, even in death she had to look her best.

If it was not so unthinkable, it might have seemed to a detached observer (had there been one there) that, as the figure bent to touch Cindy, the shoulders were shaking slightly; that she was, in fact, laughing.

But of course, that was unthinkable.

The figure touched Cindy and passed on.

*

Denny was the first to awake. He stood up shakily and looked around at the carnage. 'Oh God!' he gasped.

'What happened?'

Denny turned. It was Stiles.

'I think everyone's dead,' said Denny sardonically. 'I could be wrong of course. Maybe they're just having a kip.'

'Why aren't *we* dead?' asked Cindy emerging suddenly from through the fog.

Denny looked intently at her. 'Good question,' he said eventually. 'Why just us three?'

'You think Tamar's behind this?' said Stiles, who was prepared to believe Tamar capable of anything.'

Denny shrugged. 'The thing is,' he said. I think I *was* dead. And Tamar just doesn't have that kind of power. Not to raise the dead'

'Who does?'

'Well,' Hecaté does,' said Cindy unexpectedly. 'Only she's not allowed to use it.'

'Not allowed?' asked Denny.

'The other gods …' began Cindy.

'Ha!' said Denny. '*What* other gods?'

'Ah.'

'Wait a minute,' said Stiles. 'Are you saying that *Hecaté* did this?' That my wife can *raise* the *dead*?'

'Standard godly power,' said Denny. 'But we don't *know* it was her.'

'It could have been Eugene,' said Cindy. 'Angelic intervention.'

'He'd be thrown out of Heaven,' said Denny. 'Again.'

'He'd do it for me,' said Cindy stubbornly.

The fog was beginning to lift, and the ghastly scene was taking on a disturbing clarity in the early morning light. Cindy shivered.

'Yes,' said Denny. 'Let's go home.'

* * *

The house was deserted. That is, all the recent guests had departed, but Hecaté was still there, waiting in the hallway calmly with Jacky on her knees.

The changeling bounded over to Cindy and grasped her firmly round the neck when they arrived and Hecaté, rather more sedately embraced Stiles leaving Denny feeling rather adrift and alone. Wasn't anyone glad to see *him*?

'Where's Tamar?' he asked, more to himself really, he was not actually expecting an answer, but Hecaté looked awkward.

'Ah,' she said. 'I'd better show you. You are not going to like it,' she added.

Denny felt his stomach sink in anticipated horror. But it was worse than he imagined.

Hecaté held up the familiar bottle and sighed. 'She's in here,'

'*What*?' Denny was more furious than he had ever been in his life. It was because he was afraid. He took the bottle gingerly in shaking hands and looked at it in revulsion. Tamar's prison.

'Why?' he managed to whisper.

'She knew you were going to die,' explained Hecaté gently. 'She made a bargain. Your lives for her freedom.'

'*You*, you knew about this?'

'Yes, I was the conduit. I brought you back. Part of the bargain.'

Denny sat down suddenly. There was no chair behind him so he just sat on the floor. He suddenly felt as if he had no strength in his body. The world drained away, and he was alone in the dark. Of all the things that had happened this was the worst.

He looked at the bottle. 'Go away,' he said. His voice seemed to be coming from a long way off. 'Leave us alone.'

Hecaté nodded. 'I think she would have wanted *you* to let her out,' she said. 'That's why I did not do it.' she turned to leave.

Denny looked up suddenly. 'Don't tell the others,' he said.

Hecaté hesitated for a moment then said. 'As you wish.'

* * *

Tamar emerged from the bottle yawning and stretching and apparently unconcerned about her self-inflicted plight. Until you looked at her eyes.

'That's better,' she said flippantly then she saw Denny's face. 'Oh.'

'It's just us,' he told her in hollow tones. 'You can drop the act.'

'It's not an act,' she said. 'I'm fine, really.'

Denny moved like a snake grabbing her wrist and dragging the sleeve back to reveal the manacles there.

Tamar winced.

'*Fine* are you?' he snarled. 'You're a *slave*!'

'It could have been worse,' she said. 'I'm *your* slave. I'd rather be that than … well … I didn't want you to die.'

Denny sagged abruptly. He looked as if his insides had been ripped out. It is a fair bet that this was how he felt too. He knew instinctively that he could not make this right. A deal had been struck. If he wished her free and broke the deal, he and the others would all go back to being dead. It was infuriating.

'Who did you make this bargain with anyway?' he said.

She had been hoping he would not ask this; she had no choice but to answer him. He was the boss now.

Even so, she hedged. 'Are you sure you want to know?' she asked.

'*Tell* me.'

Tamar bowed her head obediently, and Denny was suddenly filled with remorse.

'I'm sorry,' he said. 'I didn't mean … I forgot; it's been so long. *Don't* tell me then, I mean unless you want to. I won't order you, is what I'm getting at.'

Tamar smiled. 'No wonder I fell in love with you,' she said.

'And don't try to soften me up either,' said Denny.

Still Tamar hesitated and suddenly it came to Denny in a flash.

'*Hecaté,*' he said. 'It was Hecaté, wasn't it?'

'I asked her, yes,' said Tamar.

'And *she* bargained to give up your freedom?' Denny could hardly believe it.

'It doesn't work like that,' said Tamar. 'She had no choice. If I hadn't given something up she wouldn't have been able to do it. It's the way it is. And I *needed* her to do it. It was my choice. Don't blame her.'

'I don't,' said Denny meaningfully. 'You could talk a dwarf out of drinking, a mermaid out of swimming, a …'

'… A woman out of letting the man she loves die,' finished Tamar.

'Really?' said Denny bitterly. 'Which one of us did you have in mind?'

~ Chapter Eighteen ~

THE GYPSIES ALL appeared to have gone. The camp was deserted anyway, and it looked as if something bad had happened here.

'We are sure that they *were* gypsies?' said Stiles. 'I mean, considering who their king was.'

'Oh, yes,' said Tamar. 'They were, at least most of them anyway. Finvarra just took over because they had power he could use. I'm *almost* certain,' she added.

'Do you think they knew who he was?'

'I have no idea,' she shrugged.

'What power?' said Cindy. 'I know that gypsies use magic, but Faerie magic is much more powerful.'

'Hmm,' said Tamar. 'I wonder. He must have thought they had *something*.'

'You mean you don't know,' pointed out Denny. 'They're all gone now anyway, so who cares? Let's get out of here.'

'Yes Master,' said Tamar automatically. Denny frowned, but no one seemed to notice.

'Never mind,' he said.

Stiles stirred up some debris with his foot. He thought he saw a gleam – something shiny. He reached down and picked it up.

'Hey,' he called them over. 'What this?'

It was a strange looking thing. A sort of open glove made out of bright silver filigreed metal. A ring for each finger was attached by wires to a vambrace that fitted up the arm and in the centre, where it would sit in the palm, was a large green jewel.

On the vambrace there were symbols.

Hecaté shook her head. 'This is a very old language' she said. 'Denny?'

He took it and studied it. 'Druidic runes,' he said. 'I can make out the word "god" or it might be "avatar".' He shook his head. 'I'd need my reference books.'

He handed it back to Stiles and before Denny could stop him Stiles slipped it over his hand.

'*No*,' yelled Denny alarmingly. 'Take it off, take it *off*.'

It was too late; it was not coming off. They all watched in horrified fascination as it put out tendrils into Stiles's skin. His arm went stiff, and it was possible to see the tendrils extending under the skin further up his arm in a moving fretwork. Stiles went grey. 'Oh shit!' he said.

Then his arm relaxed, and it seemed to be over. Except that the thing now seemed to be permanently attached to Stiles's hand and arm. His arm now looked as if he were wearing a gauntlet made of wires, and it shone in the sunlight.

Stiles was still staring at his arm in horror when Denny said. 'Well, that was a bloody stupid thing to do wasn't it?' and stalked off angrily.

'What's up with *him*?' said Cindy as Tamar hurried after him. 'He's been like that ever since we all came back – you know from the dead or whatever. Looks like he'd be glad he isn't dead. *I* am.'

Hecaté looked guiltily at her feet.

'There's nothing more to see here,' said Stiles briskly. 'Denny's right – on both counts – it *was* a bloody stupid thing to do, and we *should* get out of here now.'

'Are you okay then?' asked Cindy.

'That remains to be seen,' said Stiles. 'But I feel all right so far anyway.'

He looked up sharply. 'Faeries!' he said.

'Where?' said Hecaté looking around.

'Over there in the trees.' And he pointed a finger from which a blinding shaft of light shot out into the shadows accompanied by a distant shrieking then quiet.

There was a stunned silence, during which Stiles looked bemusedly at his loaded finger.

'Oh shit!' he said again. That seemed to cover it.

* * *

'Denny!'

He had his back to her and would not turn round.

'Denny please, we can't go on like this.'

Stony silence reigned. Denny hunched his shoulders, clenched his fists but said nothing.

Denny ...?

'Do you hate me?' he said suddenly. 'Is that what it is?'

'*What*?'

'You gave up everything I gave you,' he said, and he was sure he was being childish and nasty. 'There must have been another way,' he added.

Tamar was aghast. He had never talked like this before. Denny *had* given her her freedom, but he never *ever* mentioned it – *never*. Never expected gratitude for anything he did. *Was* she ungrateful? Did he really think so?

'I didn't do this lightly,' she said defensively. 'I had to.'

'Why?'

'Because you were going to *die*. Do you get that?'

'In a war that *you* started,' Denny pointed out unreasonably.

'*I* didn't start it,' she said. 'The Faeries ...'

'*You* put together an army,' he said. '*You* said we should fight, and I'm not saying that you weren't right – you were. But ...'

He turned. 'You *knew* what would happen. You planned for it.' he sighed. 'I just want to know what the hell is going on. There's more to this. I *know* you – remember? You didn't do all this just so we could fight and die and achieve nothing. And you didn't just decide to give up your freedom at the last minute because you couldn't hack it. You're up to something. You planned the whole thing, and it's time to let me in on it, don't you think?

'If I knew why,' he said quietly. 'I might be able to handle this better. I need to know why.'

'Yes,' she said. 'You do don't you.'

'I could *order* you to tell me,' he told her. 'But I won't do that. It's wrong, and besides … it's, well it's *you,* isn't it. You know what I mean?'

'Yes,' she said 'I know.'

'So …?'

'I did it to give us an advantage, that's all. There's no way this is going to be won by fighting. She knows it, but she doesn't know that *we* know it. I gave her what she expected, and now that she thinks we're all dead she'll let her guard down.'

'All?'

'I slipped off her radar when I went back into the bottle. It's the will she can detect you see, the free will of the mind. And anyway, she has no idea what I really am. She thinks – *thought* – I was a witch or something.'

'And now that her guard is down?'

'There's nothing more powerful than the combination of a Djinn and her Master. Alone, I was out of my depth but together we can't lose.'

'You were never alone,' said Denny sadly. 'I'm sorry that you didn't realise that.'[*]

'This is different,' she said.

'It certainly *is*,' he agreed ironically.

'I meant … What the hell was that?'

* * *

---

[*] When Tamar was freed from the bottle, although she retained her powers she technically became a mortal, which meant that the *strength* of her powers was necessarily diminished. She could, for example, die – if someone killed her hard enough

'What do you mean, it's probably nothing to worry about? His *eyes* were glowing!'

Denny shrugged. 'I'll translate the text on the arm band,' he offered indifferently. Tamar, he mused, had not really changed all that much as a result of her ... what would you call it, re-enslavement? At least not on the surface of it – she still acted the same way anyway. If he had not *known*, he wondered, would he have guessed?

'I need a drink,' he said and stalked off.

She did not even *try* to stop him.

'Oh, yes,' he thought. 'I *would* have guessed.'

Stiles himself was the least worried of any of them. He felt fine, more than fine actually and was, therefore, disinclined to argue with recent events. At last, he had a power. He had not exactly been hankering after supernatural powers and it was not as if he had been treated any differently for being the only one without. He had always known he had a contribution to make. But he *had* wondered what it would be like, and he *had* been aware of the difference, it just had not bothered him.

He was being treated differently now though. Which was ironic really, when you came to think about it. Everyone – except Denny he noticed – was stepping on eggshells around him. If he had not known better, he would have said they were afraid. Whether they were afraid *of* him or *for* him, was hard to say.

The problem, according to Tamar, was that they had no idea where his new powers had come from or what kind of power it was. They had been down this road before, she pointed out, when Denny had found the Athame. The truth was they were all getting a little nervous of Stiles. Denny had shown definite signs of being taken over by an evil nature during the early part of his guardianship of the Athame. Stiles, while he did not appear to be evil exactly, was manifesting powers that seemed to the others to be distinctly Faerie like.

It had almost been too late by the time Tamar had discovered Denny's slippery slope toward evil. She did not intend to make the same mistake twice. That was why she had to make Denny see how important it was to find out about the ... glove thingy. He was just going to have to get over himself.

* * *

Even Cindy had noticed that Denny was drinking pretty heavily at the moment. And he was not the friendly amiable drunk that he had once been; he had become a surly drunk, moody and unapproachable. Tamar marched into the dining room, a place which, at the moment anyway, angels would fear to tread.

At first, it seemed to be empty then a figure detached itself from the shadows in the corner. He had a bottle in his hand and was lurching slightly. He regarded the bottle venomously for a moment then hurled it into the fireplace where it smashed satisfyingly.

Tamar sighed and picked up her bottle from the hearth 'That never works you know,' she said.

'I know,' said Denny. 'That's the fifth time I've tried it. Today anyway,' he added.

Tamar waved a surreptitious hand and sobered Denny up instantly.[*]

'What did you do that for?' he asked indignantly.

'Jack needs your help,' she said bluntly. 'Your *friend*,' she added slyly acerbic. 'The one who risked his life in the Faerie castle to save you. *Remember?*

'What about him?' said Denny. 'He's all right isn't he?'

'He's ... not himself,' said Tamar uncertainly.

'Who is around here?'

'Denny!' she said warningly.

'All right, all right.' He shifted his persona and became ... well, himself again. 'The engraving said something about an Avatar,' he continued. 'I'll need to ...'

'Avatar?' interrupted. 'What's that? Is it anything like a Faerie?'

'What? No, why would you say that?'

---

[*] She used to use a foul potion for this, but that was just to teach him a lesson. Now she was in a hurry

'Jack's acting awfully … Faerie like. You haven't noticed?'

'Okay, I'll get right on it,' he said. 'And … I'm sorry. I've been a bit …'

'Upset?'

'Yeah well… that's as good a word as any I suppose.'

* * *

It was good to see Denny back at the computer console; it made things seem almost normal (as normal as things get around here anyway) Tamar felt.

Stiles had held out his wrist co-operatively to let Denny copy down the runes.

'Stop it,' said Denny as he scribbled on his pad.

'What?' said Stiles, innocently.

'Changing the runes,' said Denny. 'I can *see* you, you know? I'm not *deaf.*'

'Blind,' said Tamar automatically.

'I wasn't doing it,' protested Stiles. 'It does it all the time.'

Denny narrowed his eyes. Stiles was lying he was sure. For one thing, the runes were not exactly changing; it was only his perception of them, as if he had oil in his eyes. Had he been an ordinary human, he would never have noticed.

'We can't trust him anymore,' he realised with a shock. He looked at Tamar with a startled expression.

She nodded; it was what she had been trying to tell him.

Eventually, though, Denny thought he had got enough to begin researching the runes. The results were surprising even by their standards.

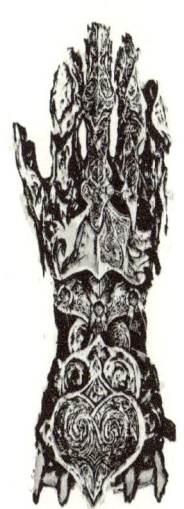

~ Chapter Nineteen ~

LONG AGO, THERE lived an ancient race of peoples known as the Tuatha De Danann. These were the people of the god Leir who inhabited the world before the coming of man. When the men arrived, they battled the Tuatha De Danann and forced them to retreat underground where they are believed to have lived in hollowed out hills.

Their descendants became known as the Sidhe.

Leir, on returning to the world of men, saw the descendants of his people and was ashamed for they had become feckless and cruel.

So, he took the four great treasures of the Tuatha De Danann, the Spear of Lugh, the Stone of Fal and the Sword of Nuada and the Dagda's Cauldron and he melted the spear and the sword in the cauldron and forged a gauntlet by plunging his living hand into the molten metal and in his palm was the stone. As the metal cooled, all Leir's power was transferred into the stone through the steel. And he wrote upon the gauntlet he had made. *Ane livinge man who bareth this steel shalle be thee Avatar of thee great Leir that his powere on earthe shalle nevere bee loste.*[*]

---

[*] Leir's spelling was terrible. All gods are like this. If it's them writing it then it

For he knew already that the power of the old gods was waning on earth, his people were all gone and all that were left were the Sidhe who he utterly rejected. And so he chose Humankind to receive his power and charged them that they must rid the world of the Sidhe. And the first to wear the gauntlet was Oman, Chief of the Gaels – sons of Mil, also known as Milesians. And in time the gauntlet passed to the druids, and the witch clans also had their custody of the power of Leir, and the Sidhe were defeated – for a time.

Then time passed, and knowledge was lost, and the gauntlet of Leir passed into the unknown and was forgotten. And the Sidhe returned, and they were angry.

Denny clapped Stiles on the back. 'Congratulations mate,' he said heartily. 'Your first time out and you've made god.'

He looked slyly at Stiles and added. 'But of course, you knew that already didn't you?'

The others looked questioningly at Stiles.

He shrugged. 'I had an idea,' he admitted. 'I can feel his thoughts – sort of, but I can't make head nor tail of them mostly.' He looked at Denny apprehensively. 'You don't mind?' he asked.

'Mind?' said Denny perplexed. 'Why should I mind – Oh, I see, because I'm only a …. Well, whatever I am. No I don't mind.'

'He has the power of a Djinn,' said Tamar. 'Dependant on no one. He's still more powerful than you are even if it doesn't sound as good.'

'I wasn't going to say anything,' said Denny. 'It seemed – tactless.' And he glared at Tamar.

'Yes,' she said unconcernedly. 'It's in bad taste to gloat, but that's why I did it *for* you. Sometimes things just need putting in perspective.'

'Shut up,'

'Yes Master … oops.'

must be right, right? This explains a lot about "Olde Englishe"]

Stiles raised an eyebrow but said nothing.

'How does it work then?' asked Cindy getting them back on track.

Stiles hesitated. 'I *think* it's connected to my brain through the central nervous system,' he said. 'When I put it on, I could feel it spreading through me – really weird feeling, by the way – anyway, I just have to think something and the gauntlet does it.'

'Your mind relays the instructions to the gauntlet?' said Denny.

'Yes, *I'm* not doing anything, it's the gauntlet that does it, I just tell it what to do. It's borrowed power. I won't live forever, and when I die the gauntlet will come off ready to be passed on.'

'An Avatar,' said Tamar. 'That's not the same as being a god then?'

'It means that he's the personification of a god, or the *idea* of a god,' said Denny.

'I am the living embodiment of the concept of belief that was the god Leir,' said Stiles somewhat pompously. 'I have the powers attributed to him and the memories, although they are somewhat nebulous, of his time as a sentient being, before he died.'

'In other words,' said Denny, translating. 'Leir's in there somewhere.'

'I am me, and also him,' said Stiles.

'Then he isn't dead, is he?' said Cindy. 'Not really. He found a way to carry on.'

'Can you control it – him, I mean?' said Tamar.

'It's not like that,' said Stiles. 'I'm not a split personality. Leir's aims in passing on his power were not selfish. I just remember him. He's not me – or I'm not him – whatever.'

He turned to Denny. 'Help me out here,' he said. 'I know *you* understand. When you took the Athame, you got the powers of the demon, but you were still *you*, right?'

'No,' said Denny.

'Oh, that's right,' said Stiles temporarily derailed.

'And was it you or Leir that tried to stop us from finding all this out?' said Tamar suspiciously.

'It was the gauntlet itself,' said Stiles, 'protecting itself.'

'But I thought it took it's instructions from you,' she countered. 'And why didn't you tell us yourself about all this?' she continued mercilessly.

'I don't know,' he said weakly. 'I just *couldn't* tell you for some reason. I felt peculiarly inhibited about it, like it was this big secret.' He brightened up a little. 'But it's okay now that you know.'

Tamar shook her head. 'How do we even know it's *you* we're talking to now?' she said.

'You'll just have to trust me,' said Stiles desperately.

Tamar looked sadly at him. 'We can't,' she said.

* * *

The whole gang was in a hitherto unknown state of discord. Denny was still angry with Tamar, with Stiles too, and not for hiding his new power either. He had forgiven them both for what had happened in the woods of course, but it rankled. What made it worse was their uncertainty at the time about whether or not it had been real. They should have *known*.

He was also being rather cold with Hecaté, although he knew that this was unfair. But he could not bring himself to talk to her in case he lost his temper and everyone found out. That it was important that no one knew, was something that Denny felt strongly about, but, if pushed, he could not have said why.

Tamar was frustrated with Denny, why could he not *understand?* She also had an unsettling feeling that he had not forgiven her for her indiscretion with Stiles in the woods, even though it was not her fault. Certain remarks that he had made, in his anger over the fact that she had become a Djinn again, had made her fear that he was indulging a belief that she had more than friendly feelings for Stiles. That he had not forgiven her, or perhaps no longer trusted her.

No one in the house trusted Stiles at the moment. He had told too many lies recently and had received a considerable power boost, the effects of which were still unclear. Who knew what he might do, or even if he were still himself.

Even Hecaté was uncertain of him; he was not acting like himself even with her. She also felt terribly guilty every time she met Denny's eye and was hurt by the way he was treating her, hurt and angry. How dare he make her feel like this?

Stiles himself was feeling isolated and uneasy. It seemed that he had paid a high price for his new abilities. The others could have told him that it was always so. Not that he blamed them for being cautious. As, he believed, the world's most suspicious man, he himself would have done no less. But still … surely a *little* support and understanding would not have been too much to ask. Instead, it seemed they had deserted him and he was left feeling angry and resentful.

As for Cindy, she was not unaware of the tensions swirling around her and, even though she was the only one in the house that no one was angry with or wary of, it was having its effect on her. She herself was annoyed with everyone, because no one would tell her what the hell was going on.

She sensed that, although they had all come to terms with Jacky, they were still uncertain of him. And no one seemed to care that her real child was still missing. They were too busy worrying about other things. Things that they apparently did not care to share with her.

She had always felt the least important in the gang. The least liked or respected and the least needed. The one who, if she disappeared, would not be missed, at least not much.

Denny treated her with bare tolerance or at best distant courtesy (the best of a bad bunch, she thought, and yet he hurt her the most for some reason). Tamar ignored her, and they all thought she was too stupid to be borne at times.

She had never really analysed these feelings before. She had thought she was unhappy because Eugene had left her alone. But now that things were so bad around here, she had had time to think. Eugene had *not* left her alone; he had left her with a whole mob of people who were supposed to be her friends – and she was still alone.

Cindy made up her mind. She lifted the changeling out of his cot. 'Come on Kiddo,' she said. 'Let's get out of here,'

The changeling gurgled happily and wrapped chubby arms around her neck.

'At least there's still *one* person around here who loves me,' thought Cindy.

And, although she would have died before she admitted it, she was not so much thinking of Eugene as of Denny.

~ Chapter Twenty ~

IT HAD BEEN A week since they had returned and there was still no sign of Tamar's plan – if she had even had one beyond making sure that no one died.

The Faerie Queen was known to have rebuilt her palace and was presiding over a reign of terror from there, and still Tamar did nothing.

There was the question now, of course, of how Stiles's new powers could be factored in. As Denny had pointed out, they had gone to the abandoned gypsy camp in hopes of finding something that might help, knowing full well that Finvarra had used their power and he had had control of the portal stones. But it had to be admitted that what they had had in mind was something more along the lines of something to use on the stones instead of witch (or as it turned out druid) blood.

There was an unspoken decision among all of them not to engage the Faeries again until they had something pretty solid to use against them. Something, in fact, that could not fail.

There was nothing. Unless it turned out that Stiles's new powers were the key and they could not be sure of that yet.

And they were safe here for the time being …

There was a scuffle in the hall. A bewildered Faerie had broken in and found itself facing the kind of odds that Faeries tried to avoid i.e. one person but with a sword and in a very bad temper.

Tamar waved the sword threateningly at the Faerie, and it backed nervously toward the door. Denny watching over the banister thought it looked rather foxy faced although it was clearly trying hard to look better. It put Denny in mind of the Queen.

It was having no effect on Tamar, even though it did look rather like Denny. Finally, it gave up and fled out the door. Tamar pursued it. It stood on the step shaking and gasping. Tamar did not move for a second, and the Faerie asked. 'You're just going to let me go?'

'No,' said Tamar. 'I just didn't want you to bleed on the carpet.' And she struck.

Denny looked thoughtful as he walked back up the stairs unobserved.

'Denny's in a pretty bad mood these days,' said Stiles coming up behind her.'

'Yes,' said Tamar, 'well.' She did not turn round.

Stiles nodded. 'I know you don't trust me anymore,' he said. 'But I think you should listen to me anyway.'

Tamar turned round slowly. 'Okay then,' she said. 'What?'

Stiles nodded as if she had just answered a question. 'Thought so,' he said.

Tamar frowned. 'What are you talking about?' she snapped.

Denny called Tamar from up the stairs, and she instantly made to go.

'That,' said Stiles. 'You *have* to go don't you?'

'Denny wants me,' she said evasively.

'And he's the Master now,' agreed Stiles. 'I *am* a policeman,' he added in answer to her wary expression. 'I notice things.' He lifted his hands. 'No freaky powers I promise, I had my suspicions before I ever got ... "Avatared" and well ...' he took her unresisting arm gently. 'Looks like I'm not the only one to have recently acquired some new wrist-wear. He drew back her sleeve as Denny had done to reveal the manacle.

'*Tamar.*'

'Yes *Master?*' said Stiles. 'That was a bit of a giveaway you know.'

Still Tamar said nothing.

Denny came bounding down the stairs 'Tam … oh!' he stopped short as he took in the scene. 'She can't tell you about it,' he said to Stiles. 'I – um – told her not to.' He had the grace to look embarrassed about this, so Stiles did not comment. He just *looked*.

'Why?' he said.

'It doesn't matter now,' said Denny. 'I didn't want Cindy to know either.' He felt this was a point worth making – there was enough bad feeling around as it was. 'Where *is* Cindy anyway?' he added. 'I haven't seen her all day.'

'Sulking in her room,' said Stiles dismissively. 'Don't change the subject.'

'Cindy doesn't sulk,' said Tamar obediently.

'Anyway, she always comes down at one to feed the … Jacky,' said Denny and it's nearly two.'

Stiles was being tag-teamed by them, and he knew it. He gave it one last try. 'This is *me* guys,' he said. 'I promise. Please just tell me what's going on.'

Denny sighed. 'Think about it mate,' he said. And Stiles smiled in relief at the re-introduction of this familiarity.

'How do you think Hecaté managed to bring us all back?'

'Nothing's free,' put in Tamar.'

'Oh God,' said Stiles as this sunk in.'

'Don't talk to yourself,' said Denny. 'I'll think you've lost your mind.'

Stiles gave a weak smile at this sally.

'That's why we didn't tell you,' said Tamar.

'So now we *all* know,' said Denny. 'Except Cindy. I suppose we'd better tell her too.'

Hecaté appeared in the room. 'You will have to find her first,' she said. 'Cindy has left the house. She took the little one with her and all of her clothes too. She appears to have left for good.'

Denny groaned. 'More trouble,' he said.

* * *

Cindy was barrelling along an eerily deserted motorway on stolen motorbike (stolen from Denny actually although he rarely used it) with the wind whipping through her hair (witches do not need crash helmets). She did not know where she was going, or how far. Just so long as it was far, far away from Den ... the others. She could have gone farther and faster by teleporting, but everyone knew that the Faeries could sense witch magic (well, for a given value of *everyone*) so it just was not worth it. And anyway, Tamar could easily track her that way. She did not want any trouble, not with Faeries or with Tamar, if Tamar caught up with her it would definitely lead to awkward questions.

For the moment, anyway she was happy. She felt curiously free. Later, when she came to analyse her feelings, she knew she would feel both lonely and wretched. But so what? She had felt lonely and wretched at home and, deep in her heart, she knew very well the reason why.

It was at this moment that her mind decided to throw up the inconvenient memory that Tamar, of all people, had remembered Mother's Day that year and had even provided a card and flowers, ostensibly from Jacky. Even Hecaté had not remembered.

But Tamar *had*. Cindy just could not figure it out.

The small bundle strapped to her back gurgled happily, and Cindy was grateful for that at least. At least he was not frightened. On the contrary, he seemed to be having the most fun she had ever known him to have. Thank God, there were no Plod about. Cindy winced as she thought this. "Plod" was a Denny word and one that a few years ago she would not have dreamed of uttering, even in the privacy of her head.

But then, she had changed and in greater ways than this.

What a pity nobody seemed to have noticed.

* * *

'*Why* would she leave?' this was Tamar, she sounded angry – which meant that she was worried.

Stiles shrugged, and Hecaté looked perplexed, but Denny looked thoughtful.

Tamar would, at one time have pounced on this and demanded to know what he was thinking.

Fortunately, Stiles was there to pick up the slack. 'What do *you* think?' he asked Denny.

'I think she's sick and tired of us,' said Denny. 'And I don't blame her either.'

'But it's not *safe* out there,' said Tamar ignoring the implication.

'It's not safe in *here* either,' said Denny. 'Not anymore.'

'Well … *you'll* have to go and get her,' said Tamar in a fair imitation of her usual high-handed manner. 'It has to be you,' she added. 'You're the only one she'll listen to.'

'Me?' said Denny innocently.

'Oh come on, we all know she has a crush on you.'

'Only now and then,' said Denny vaguely, before he had time to think.

'So? Boss her about a bit.'

Denny blushed. He had not realised she had noticed. But of *course* she had, he realised. She probably thought it was funny. And that was the problem wasn't it? None of them took Cindy very seriously. No wonder she had gone. He suddenly felt terribly guilty. He had more reason than anyone here to feel this way. He had a horrible feeling that this was his fault – well, well *mainly* his fault. But surely, Cindy had not been …

He became aware that Tamar was looking quizzically at him.

'All right, all right.' He gave in. 'But I want Jack to come too, she's bound to have covered her tracks. I need a detective.' He did not want to face Cindy alone. That was the truth of it, if he was honest.

Stiles saluted ironically. 'Yessir,' he said. 'At your service sah?'

'She won't be all that hard to find *surely*?' said Tamar. 'This is *Cindy* we're talking about.'

'Don't underestimate her,' said Denny. 'She's not stupid you know.'

'No she is not.' said Hecaté. 'She really is not.'

Tamar looked bewilderedly at both of them.

'She's *not*?'

* * *

'See I told you,' said Denny. 'She took my bike; I *knew* she wouldn't use magic. Too risky.'

'What do you think she was afraid of?' said Tamar ironically, 'me or the Faeries?'

'Both probably.'

'Hmm.' Stiles was thinking. 'She probably went north then. It's clear that way. The Faeries are all the other way.'

'They've closed the roads off to the north,' said Denny.

'Exactly, said Stiles, 'a nice clear run. She's a *witch* – remember? If she even knows the traffic laws, you can bet she doesn't apply them to herself.'

'Unless she thinks that we'll think of that,' said Denny.

'Hah!' said Tamar. 'That would be graduate level thinking for Cindy.'

'Tamar's right,' said Stiles, 'Cindy may not be stupid, but let's not give her *too* much credit.'

'It's far more likely that she doesn't think we'll bother chasing her,' said Denny severely.

'Hecaté?' said Stiles. 'Can't *you* sense her?'

'No, I cannot. She is moving too fast.'

'Okay,' said Denny carefully, 'in what direction?'

Hecaté concentrated. 'North north east,' she said.

'That's the motorway,' said Denny. 'Come on Jack. Let's get her back before she does something ...'

'Stupid?' supplied Tamar.

~ Chapter Twenty One ~

IT WAS GETTING dark, and the hills were turning a misty purple colour; it was getting cold.

Cindy skidded the motor bike to an inexpert stop and blinked. The hills were doing strange things in the foggy twilight, moving nearer and farther, bowing and rippling like thin silk in a breeze. Suddenly a hill detached itself from the others and stood up in the shape of an exceptionally large man.

Now Cindy had seen some pretty astounding things over the last few years, but this was a bit too much for her. She whimpered and tried to convince herself she was dreaming. The man stood against the skyline, bigger than King Kong, stretched arms several miles long, and said in a loud, booming voice that carried over the countryside. 'THAT ART BETTYR.'

Then he spotted Cindy.

Cindy remembered herself and checked Jacky who was not, as she had expected, rigid with terror but rather seemed, not only calm, but actually happy.

She did not have time to wonder about this, as the colossal figure was walking upright down the steep slope of the hill in a manner that surely no human being could have managed.

Contrary to the usual way of natural perspective, however, he seemed to be diminishing in size the closer he came to her until he stood before her hardly any taller than she was. There was no question of running away; her legs were paralysed. Her tongue was not though.

'Who the hell are you?' she managed a little shakily but reasonably calmly in the circumstances.

'You should go home,' he told her. 'It isn't safe for witches out here. She will find you.'

He turned his attention to Jacky who gurgled happily. 'Ah,' he said. 'My son. You have taken good care of him I see.' And he reached a hand out to the baby.

Cindy snatched him away angrily. Suddenly she knew who this was.

'Finvarra!' she said wonderingly. 'Tamar said you were dead.'

'Do you really think that I can be killed so easily?' he said. 'I who have walked this earth for a thousand years.'

'*I don't care*!' yelled Cindy. 'Where the hell is *my* son?'

'He is safe,' said Finvarra.

'Where is …'

Finvarra took her gaze and held it; there was a terrible darkness in his eyes. There was a moment of dizziness then the world fell away, and everything went black.

* * *

She awoke to find an anxious Denny bending over her. 'Cindy?' he was saying. 'Cindy, are you all right? What happened?' he lifted her gently onto her feet. 'Did you have an accident?'

'Finvarra,' she managed.

'Denny,' he told her, not understanding.

'No, he was here, where's Jacky?'

'He's fine,' Denny assured her. 'Jack took him home What do you mean he was here? Finvarra's dead.'

'Not dead, I saw him. He … he …'

Okay, okay, never mind for now, as long as you're all right. You can tell me later – at home.'

There was no gainsaying that tone of voice when he used it. It meant you did what he said and did not argue.

He never asked her why she had left.

He did not want to know, she thought, which meant he had a good idea, he just did not want to hear it. Well, that was all right with her. She did not want to say it.

The journey back was the most terrifying and exhilarating experience of Cindy's life. She had thought she had ridden the bike pretty fast, but Denny drove everything from a truck to a pedal boat at what Tamar referred to as warp speed.

Stiles had taken the car that he and Denny had driven together, and he drove sedately home, aware that he had what, for want of a better description, he called a "kiddie" in the back, and without a child seat to strap him into.

Which meant that Denny and Cindy *should* have been home long before him.

* * *

Denny skidded to a halt in a much more professional manner than she had done she could not help noticing admiringly. And for a similar reason – there was someone in the road. A woman or at least a female person. It was the Faerie Queen.

Denny dismounted slowly and menacingly and stood rocking on his heels looking at her in a manner that Cindy fervently hoped he never used on her.

Then, suddenly, Cindy knew what she had to do.

She teleported straight for the stones

Without missing a beat, Denny followed her, and hot on his heels was the Queen.

Cindy only had a few seconds lead, but it was enough. As the Faerie Queen re-materialised Cindy grabbed her, pulled her through the stones and held her there.

For once, she had completely confounded Denny. 'What the hell ...?' he began.

The Faerie Queen pulled free from Cindy and ran. Ran away farther into the Faerie realm. It was either that or face Denny, and no one would do that at the moment. He was confused and, therefore, pissed off and ready to take it out on anyone he did not particularly like. The Faerie Queen qualified.

It was about to get much worse for Denny.

'She'll get out again,' said Denny, 'unless we guard it.'

'No,' said Cindy, grimly determined. 'It ends here. 'She took a large kitchen knife that she kept secreted about her person at all times. Mystic Athames were all very well, but every witch knows that sometimes you can't beat a good, sharp bread knife.

Denny got the point at once, but he asked the question anyway as if it was part of an invisible script. 'What are you doing?'

He tried to get to her but was stopped by an invisible barrier at the stones. It seemed that Cindy had a will of her own when she wanted to. Denny could probably have broken through in time. But he sensed that he did not have *enough* time.

'Sealing the portal behind her,' said Cindy. 'Don't try to stop me. You can't anyway. She came for *you*. She was looking for you and, as soon as you left the protection of the house, she *found* you. She'll never stop. As long as she's here you'll never be able to go out, you'll never be free of her. She's made up her mind to have you. But I can stop her, right here, right now; there'll never be a better chance. The blood of a witch on the stones.'

'You *can't!*' he said. 'We'll find another way.'

'There *is* no other way,' she said. 'Let me do this ... for you.'

'Why?' he said helplessly. He pushed futilely against the barrier.

Cindy smiled wistfully as she raised the knife to her neck. 'I love you,' she said sadly, and struck.

Blood splashed on the stones. The barrier came down – too late.

Denny fell to his knees and howled.

* * *

Cindy awoke to find an anxious Denny bending over her. 'Cindy?' he was saying. 'Cindy, are you all right? What happened?' he lifted her gently onto her feet. 'Did you have an accident?'

Cindy stared blankly at him for a few seconds, then she rebooted her thoughts. 'I hate premonitions,' she said mysteriously.

Denny thought she must have hit her head.

Cindy replayed events as best she could in her head and then said. 'Where's Jacky?'

I love you?

'He's fine, Jack took him home What happened?'

'Finvarra's alive I saw him.'

He needs to know that part at least ... I love him?

'He's alive?'

'Yes, and since I know you're going to order me to come home with you and I'm going to agree because it's so hard to argue with you, why don't I tell everyone together about it when we get there? I think we should teleport by the way.'

I do love him; I think I always have. But it doesn't mean I'm ready to die for him. I'm not out of my mind!

'Teleport?' said Denny trying to keep up. 'What about …?'

'They can find us *anyway*,' said Cindy. 'Trust me on this.'

'At least, she can find you,' she thought, 'and that's enough. The faster we get home the better.'

'I do,' said Denny. He was thinking of the Faerie that had broken into the house. But Cindy did not know about this. He would have to tell her … everything.

'I've got a lot to tell you too,' he said.

Cindy nodded. 'It's about time,' she said.

They teleported just as the Faerie Queen appeared in the street. 'Damn,' she snapped, 'missed him again,'

* * *

The Faerie Queen had, in fact, registered Denny's reanimation almost as soon as it happened. He was still the best choice, in her view, for a consort, and she had been regularly sending agents to the house to try to get to him. Until recently though, none had been able to penetrate the safeguards around the group of people living there. It was odd; she could not sense the black haired one from whom such terrible power emanated. She had gone, it seemed, and yet ... *somehow* the power she had wielded was still there, but it was weakening. Only this day an agent had finally got as far as the inside of the house, but a power within had driven it out. Still it was a start.

And then he had left the sanctuary and exposed himself to her but again had been whisked away before she could ... it was very frustrating.

* * *

Denny was well aware that the protective power that Tamar had placed around them was weakening, and he thought he knew why. It was him. He was the Master now and he had not been giving much thought to the issue of protecting the house. He realised that he had just unconsciously relied on Tamar for – well, a lot of things actually, a lot of things that she did automatically, things he had taken for granted. But she could not do it now, not without him. The spell was wavering because her will had been removed, technically, now she had no will of her own, only his will and he clearly was not up to the job.

He had taken her for granted for the last time, he decided. Remembering all the things that needed doing all the time was a lot of effort. Women, he seemed to remember reading somewhere, were better than men at parallel processing. The best he could do was to carry on a coherent conversation about shoes while actually thinking about football. And even then, he was sure he was not fooling her. In any case, she needed to be free again if she were to function effectively. He was holding her back.

He went to find her.

* * *

Cindy had been accepted back without much comment. There really did not seem to be much to say. Tamar had been slightly taken aback to discover that Finvarra was alive again but had glossed over it with the comment that there was a lot of it about. This had led inevitably to the revelation of Tamar's new status and the reasons thereof. Cindy had been shocked but had wisely said very little about it sensing that it was a particularly sore subject with Denny. She was finding herself being rather more sensitive to Denny's moods these days. A fact which she found quietly disturbing.

She hummed as she put the counterfeit Jacky to bed and wondered vaguely where the other – she corrected herself sharply – the *real* Jacky was. It was hard to mourn for a child that she had never really known. This, for all intents and purposes, was her baby.

And she really was not too worried about the other. Finvarra had said he was safe, and she believed him. Even Denny had said that the stolen children were probably all right, and if *he* thought so then, as far as Cindy was concerned, it was probably true.

She left Jacky curled up in his cot peacefully and went up to her bedroom to brood about Denny.

* * *

Denny himself was brooding about Tamar. He was also trying vainly to find her, what he found was the bottle. He picked it up curiously. In view of what he had in mind it occurred to him for the first time to wonder what it was like inside. He concentrated.

Tamar was in there and none too pleased to see him either. 'What do you think you are doing?' she snapped.

'I was just curious,' he said lamely. 'I just realised that in all the time you were living in here before, you never once asked me over,'

He looked around him at the sumptuous furnishing (mainly cushions). 'It's nice,' he said. 'And no need to lock the door,' he added hopefully, plonking himself down on a cushion and raising his eyebrows at her suggestively.

Tamar laughed. 'Is that all you ever think about?' she said.
'Yes,' said Denny and pounced.

* * *

'I have a wish,' he began carefully after… afterwards.
'Actually, *three* wishes,' he added just so there was no mistake.

'Sure?' said Tamar. 'You know it's not always a good idea.'

'I know what I'm doing,' said Denny.

'I used to think that,' she warned him. 'And look at some of the messes I've made.'

Denny did not comment. One of the worst mistakes she had ever made in this regard had very nearly turned him into a demon.

'I wish …' he said.

And Tamar closed her eyes and prayed. Not *to* anyone of course, Tamar had met too many gods to fall for this one, but just prayed in general.

'… To be Omnipotent, Omniscient and Immortal' he said.

Tamar's eyes slammed open. 'Oh *no!*' she cried. 'I won't do it.'

'You have to.'

Tamar's eyes narrowed. 'Yes Master,' she said in chagrin. And in the blink of an eye, she was free and Denny was the Djinn. Tamar, unlike the unlamented Askphrit did not go in for showy special effects. What she *did* do was burst into tears.

'Now you know how I felt,' remarked Denny.

'Sod off,' she said.

'Quite,' agreed Denny. And because she was the Master now, he did.[*]

'Denny!' she ordered.

He came back. 'Yes Master.'

'You know I could just wish us back the other way around?' she said.

'I know,' he said. 'Master … how do I stop saying that?'

---

[*] Djinn are quite capable of nonliteral interpretation and Denny knew that Tamar had not meant this literally. He was just being awkward.

'It takes practice,' she said. 'I want to know why you did it,' she said fighting for calm.

'Because we need you at full power with free will and everything,' said Denny, 'if we're ever going to win this. Because I couldn't live with the guilt. Because 5000 years of servitude is enough. Because I know you'll find a way out of this for me far sooner than that.'

'All good points,' admitted Tamar resignedly. 'You'll hate it you know.'

'I imagine I will … Master – *shit*!'

'I mean it,' she said. 'It took me about a hundred years to acclimatise and even then I was still mad.'

That's right, cheer me up.' He gritted his teeth, but it still came out. 'Master,'

Tamar grinned. 'That's going to get on my nerves even more than yours,' she said.

'I doubt it – Master,' he said sourly.

'Djinn,' she said. 'Don't answer me, just listen. 'Djinn, I wish for you not to call me "Master" anymore,'

'Your wish is my command,' said Denny automatically. 'Thank you,' he added. 'You know I expected to feel it, the magic you know.'

'Only for the big stuff,' she said. 'You'll feel it then all right. Except you won't because I'm not going to wish anymore.'

'It's harder than you think,' said Denny. 'We'll see.'

'I *will* get you out of this,' she said ignoring, as she always did, the wisdom of experience that was not her own.

'We'll see,'

Tamar could not believe it. That Denny, that *anyone*, even Denny would do this for her. She tried to convince herself that he had not really understood what he would be giving up but it wouldn't wash. She knew damn well that he understood. She had a lot to live up to.

She was having another experience; one that only one person had ever had before in the whole history of creation as far as she knew. She had become a free Djinn. Unlimited power *and* free will. It was a heady experience. Before, when she had become free, she had technically retained her powers, but as a mortal. This was different; she felt invincible.

'And I thought I *knew* what power was,' she thought. 'I had no idea.' She just hoped it did not go to her head.

And she was the Master of *another* Djinn. Yet *more* power. 'We can't fail,' she thought.

'This is it,' she realised with a shock. 'This is what I was waiting for. Time to sort this out. Time to go after the Queen.'

* * *

'Damn I lost him.' The Queen was not really enjoying her reign of terror as much as she had hoped. Without her chosen consort, it just was not the same. And since she had set her sights on Denny, her preoccupation with finding him was becoming an obsession – which will take the fun out of anything,

Now she had lost him, that is she could not find his mind, it was as if he had simply vanished. If one of her Faeries had killed him … but no, his power was still evident, just as … and that was when she realised. Tamar was back.

She did not understand it. Were they one being? No! Then how was it that when one vanished, the other returned? The power they wielded was similar, and she had never been able to quantify it in either of them, was it, in fact, the *same* power, did they share it? Such a bond would be hard to break. But not impossible. The Faerie Queen smiled. The dark haired harridan would have to die. Now *that* sounded like fun.

* * *

Denny was watching Tamar in, well … concern, if not actual panic. The power was strobing through her. She was thrumming like a badly strung guitar. It made Denny nervous. What the hell had he done? Was this what had happened to Askphrit? No wonder he had gone mad.

Then suddenly she turned to him and smiled and the power surge faded away. 'Don't worry,' she said with that uncanny knack she had of reading his thoughts. 'I've got it under control.'

'Famous last words,' thought Denny.

* * *

When they told the others, Denny thought they took it pretty well really, for the most part anyway. Cindy, however, had blinked suspiciously bright eyes and walked away without saying a word.

'You go after her,' said Tamar to Denny. 'I know you want to.'

*

'Go away,' said Cindy.

'What's up?' countered Denny. He did not have to do what *she* told him to.

She turned round at the foot of the stairs. 'I can't believe you did that,' she said. And the tears formed in her eyes.

'Do you care about me so much?' asked Denny. He had not meant to ask this, he did not think he really wanted to know the answer, but it had just sort of come out.

'It's not that,' she lied. 'It's just … how did things get so messed up?

Denny grinned in relief. 'Hah!' he said. 'When aren't things messed up around here?'

'But never this badly. I mean you're a slave. That's pretty messed up.'

'That's Faeries for you,' he said. 'From what I've heard anyway, when they arrive things always go to hell.'

Cindy nodded. 'It was a big sacrifice,' she said meaning his.

Denny nodded. 'No bigger than the one Tamar made,' he pointed out. 'Besides, I think I did it partly out of guilt.'

'You did it entirely out of love,' said Cindy wistfully. 'You forget. I *know* you. Better than you think, I think.' She paused. 'Oh poor Cindy,' she said, her anger rising. 'She doesn't know what's going on, too thick to notice what's under her nose, but I see things too you know. It's astonishing what you can pick up when no one thinks you're important enough to hide things from.'

'No one thinks that,' said Denny defensively.

'You *all* do,' said Cindy. 'I don't blame you really, I bring it on myself. People have always treated me like that. It's the blonde hair, do you think?'

'*I've* got blonde hair.'

'Yes, but you're…'

'Ugly?' said Denny with a grin.

'No,' she answered seriously. 'No, not ugly, just … well… you're a man aren't you? And besides, you act sort of … and you … never mind.' She waved a hand. 'It doesn't matter. Do you want to see my real face?' she asked suddenly.

But Denny had learned a thing or two since taking up with Tamar.

'That *is* your real face,' he told her. And he meant it too. Wear a face long enough and it becomes your own. Like politicians and opinions.

Cindy smiled. 'One of them anyway, I meant the other one, without the magic.'

'Not at all,' said Denny. 'It won't change my opinion of you in any way. I saw Tamar's "real" face once you know.'

'You *did*?' Cindy was amazed. 'I'm amazed she let that happen,' she said.

'It *was* a sort of an accident,' admitted Denny. 'But it didn't make a difference. I never judged people on what they look like. Well, when you look like me you can't really.'

'I used to, but not anymore,' she said. 'I live in a different world now I suppose.'

'You've learned to see beyond the surface,' agreed Denny. 'It's a magical thing.'

'Like the Faerie queen,' said Cindy. 'She obviously saw something in you. I should warn you I guess. She's still after you. She knows you're alive.'

'How do you know?'

'I had a premonition about it, I meant to tell you before, but I couldn't think how to put it, sorry.'

'Well, she won't find me now,' said Denny holding up his wrists to display the manacles.

'But it's good that you told me,' he added seeing her face fall. 'Maybe I can use it somehow.'

'You're a nice guy,' said Cindy. 'Kind. You don't have to be. I'm tougher than I look.'

'You'd have to be around here,' Denny agreed.

'Around here,' she said vaguely. 'Yes, you know before I came here I never had a problem with my self-esteem. I was always the best-looking woman in the room. No other woman stood a chance against me. I mean I'm a witch. A witch among ordinary women, that was me, but now ... I'm a witch among Tamar and Hecaté. It's a lot harder.'

'You don't have to compete.'

'It's all I know,' wailed Cindy. 'All witches are competitive. We can't help it.'

'Is that why you left?' Denny was amazed at himself. In the middle of all this chaos, he was taking time out to counsel a strung out witch. He could not remember ever having such a long conversation with Cindy before. Perhaps it was necessary, though. *Someone* had to do it obviously. They could not afford to have any dead weight on board at the moment. Things were too dicey, and if Cindy decided to take off again ... He was shocked at his own cynicism. It was the Djinn, though, who was thinking like this, not Denny.

'Not precisely,' she said. 'I left because I felt like I should. No one was talking to me, and no one seemed to care about my son. I wanted to find him, but now ...' she left the sentence hanging.

Denny did not believe a word of this and was judging whether it was a good idea to say as much or not when Cindy burst out. 'You shouldn't feel so damn lonely in your own home.'

'Oh, I *did* want to find my son,' she continued in a calmer tone. 'But only, if I'm honest, because I felt like I should. The truth is I never knew that child. It's not that I don't care about what they did. I'm furious actually. But when all is said and done … *he's not my son.*'

All this might be the truth, thought Denny, but it was wide of the mark in terms of getting to whatever it was that was eating at Cindy. But he shied away from it. He did not want to know. He had a horrible feeling that it involved him, and the thought made him cringe with embarrassment. So he pulled back, as he did every time he felt as if he was getting too close to the murky waters of Cindy's feelings, whatever they were. (And it was easier not to hear it out loud, that way he could pretend he did not know.)

'You don't want to know the rest,' observed Cindy. 'That's okay. I feel better anyway.'

'I don't know why you giving up so much for her should hurt me so much,' she muttered to herself. 'You can't lose what you never had.'

Denny pretended that he had not heard.

* * *

Tamar was sitting on the bed with her eyes closed and a look of intense concentration on her face. She was looking for the Faerie Queen.

Denny had told her about his conversation with Cindy (the relevant part anyway) and she had been dismissive.

'Premonition?' she had said. 'You mean like "fortune telling"? Look deeply into my bosom, that kind of thing? Although,' she had added, 'if I catch you looking deeply into Cindy's bosom, there will be trouble.'

'You have no idea,' thought Denny.

'I can't find her,' she said snapping her eyes open.

Denny cocked an eyebrow and said nothing, clearly she was not actually talking to him, he just happened to be there.

'She isn't real you see,' Tamar confided to the bedpost. 'I think that's the problem. She's only a figment.'

Denny frowned at this. For a figment, she had certainly done a lot of damage. But he said nothing. Tamar was clearly working through some train of thought.

'I can see everything, but I can't see Faeries, because they aren't real, well they are real obviously, but not … it's like gods … they're only here because we invented them. But I *can* see the effect they're having. Ah good, so if I find the… the – *epicentre* of the trouble, that'll be her. Right!' She closed her eyes again.

Denny was amused despite the seriousness of the situation. Tamar did sound *so* funny talking to herself like a metal patient talking to the voices in her head.

'*Faeries*!' he thought, and he began to laugh at the utter ludicrousness of the situation.

The sudden sound broke Tamar's concentration, and she opened her eyes and glared at him. 'I almost had it then,' she snapped. 'Shut *up*!'

Denny lowered his eyes. 'Sorry,' he said.

She sighed. 'Who am I kidding?' she asked the world in general. 'I've got nothing. I don't understand it.' Denny realised that this was another monologue. 'Why can't I find her? I'm omniscient for God's sake'

'Maybe Jack …' began Denny, but she was not listening.

'I should have just gone after her when she went through the stones,' she said. 'She could be *anywhere* by now. At least I knew where she was then. I wish I could go back and do it again. I'd do it right this time.'

Denny covered his face with his hands. 'Your wish,' he said through gritted teeth, 'is my command.'

Tamar stared at him. 'Oops!' she said, then vanished.

~ Chapter Twenty Two ~

DENNY CURSED LOUDLY and stood flabbergasted for at least thirty seconds before he got himself together enough to follow her. Which meant he was at least thirty seconds behind events. Sometimes thirty seconds are all it takes to make all the difference in the world.

The Queen of the Sidhe backed away from Tamar nervously. In our world at least, the only power they really have is over the mind. They make you *believe* you are beaten. But Tamar *never* believed she was beaten. Even if she had still been under the Faerie thrall, it would have taken some spell to break her absolute belief in herself.

Tamar raised the sword and Queen Onagh watched it like a rabbit watching a snake, she was clearly terrified.

Then Denny came crashing through the trees. The queen raised her head and started in astonishment. Tamar was only distracted for a millionth of a second, but it was enough for the Faerie Queen. She stepped lightly aside through a gap in the stones and disappeared.

Tamar let out a howl of rage.

'*No!*' yelled Denny desperately and ran for the stones, but he was too late. Tamar had followed the queen through the portal.

She never let anything go.

Except apparently her sword, helmet and all her armour. No iron gets past the Key Stones into the Faerie realm.

Denny sighed. There really was nothing else for it. He took a deep breath (his last for some time as it turned out) and followed her in.

As Tamar stepped through the music switched off suddenly, but there were other sounds, most notably, the sound of laughter.

'Well,' she thought, looking around, 'not exactly what I had in mind, but perhaps this is even better.'

The world on the other side of the stones was nothing like the world she had left behind. This world was bright and cheerful, nauseatingly so. It reminded Tamar of a film she had once seen. The world she had left was in black and white, dreary and colourless, and this world was brightly coloured and dazzlingly attractive. What *had* that place been called? Oh yes, that was it – "Toon Town"

The sky was a soft, streaky pink and purple sunset. The grass was too green, the lakes too blue, the trees too pretty; the whole place looked like a freshly painted backdrop. Only the standing stones were the same, and they stood out, stark, murky and graceless, an imposition on the landscape, as the Faerie castle had been in the human world, ugly intruders from a harsher world.

Her throat felt strange and she found herself pawing at it, and her chest felt strangely heavy, but it was not distressing, just strange.

The Faerie queen was nowhere to be seen.

Denny appeared behind her. 'Bloody he...' then he clutched at his throat rasping and gurgling desperately.

Tamar raised an eyebrow as Denny passed out. 'No air?' she thought. 'That's interesting.'

Tamar was not really being completely callous about Denny's condition – she knew he would be all right. He just had to adjust his thinking. After all, he was a Djinn now. He did not need to breathe

This was not a real world then – new rules.

'Well,' she thought, 'I can work with that.'

She gave Denny a kick. 'Come on lazybones,' she said. 'We've got work to do.'

Denny pulled himself together and looked around. Memories flooded into his head.

'I'm still me,' he announced bizarrely. 'We're still us, I mean shouldn't we be *them*? He meant the other versions of themselves from this point in time. Tamar understood him though.

'No. They have a different future,' she said, 'the one that led us here.'

Denny thought about this. 'You mean we've created a bloody paradox?'

'No, not this time,' she said. 'It's hard to explain. 'Everything that happened stays happened. It's just that … now there are *two* presents running side by side, the one where we came back and the one where we didn't.

'*They* (us) are in the other one. The two presents will run together like parallel worlds (only not exactly) until we catch up with ourselves.' *

'But this is the past.'

'Not to us. This is the present to us now. We're separate. Just trust me, it's better this way.'

'Well,' said Denny grasping for a solid, incontrovertible fact in this morass of confusion. 'You can't change the past.'

'I'm not going to,' she said.

'Good.'

---

* Not many people can speak in brackets, but Tamar did not know this, so she did it anyway.]

'I'm going to change the present.'
'Oh.'

Away in the distance was an exact replica of the Faerie's castle that had held Denny. He shuddered at it.

He was back on his feet now and felt fine apart from a sore throat because he kept trying to breathe – he had been in the habit of it for twenty seven years after all. Tamar was faring better; she had only recently got back into the habit of breathing having not bothered for five thousand years, it having been more or less optional when she had been living in a bottle.

'That's where she'll be,' said Tamar following his gaze.

'It's a long way off,' he said squinting at it.

'Depends on your point of view,' said Tamar. 'Come on,' she added, as he looked sceptical. 'You've been doing this long enough now to know the score. Remember the deleted file? It's not real, remember, the castle is only as far away as you think it is.'

'Not real?' murmured Denny vaguely – he was saving his energy for worrying.

'Look at this place,' said Tamar with an expansive movement of her arm. 'This is,' she spat the last word, '*fairyland*!'

'It's horrible,' said Denny.

Tamar looked sideways at him. 'You noticed that?' she said. 'Good, don't get sucked in.'

Denny considered trying to convince her to leave. He was hating this place. It was so creepy. They could go back; it was probably not too late. And as for the Queen ...

'She'll be back,' said Tamar as if reading his thoughts – which she probably was. 'We *know* she will.' she added.

Denny shrugged 'I wasn't going to say anything,' he said. 'What would be the point?' he added *sotto voce*.

Tamar ignored him; she appeared to be thinking. After a few moments, she suddenly put two fingers in her mouth and let out a piercing whistle.

Almost immediately, two wild ponies galloped up to them and stood expectantly stamping their hooves.

'There we are,' said Tamar. 'Transport for two, no waiting. This place has it good points.'

Denny looked at the castle, 'I can't think of any,' he said.

Tamar looked at him from her seat on the pony's back. 'You don't have to come you know,' she said. 'I can handle this.'

Denny swung himself up onto the other pony without a word. Tamar nodded. 'Okay, then.'

As they thudded over the grass, Denny wondered what she was planning to do. If this place was not real, as she claimed – and it certainly seemed that way – then neither she nor he would be able to use their powers here. Supernatural powers never worked in places that were not part of the real world as they had both discovered to their cost before this.

The Athame would be no use here – except as an exceptionally sharp knife – and they did not have any iron.

'I could always sing again,' he thought. But as a long-term plan, this had its drawbacks.

Not that there was not magic here of course. The place reeked of it, but it was a magic that belonged to this world, Faerie magic, the kind that messes with your head. And there was no way they could use that.

And yet, he realised with a start, Tamar had already used it. They could not use their own powers to teleport to the castle, so she had used the Faerie magic to summon horses to take them there. He relaxed a little. If they could use the Faerie magic then at least they were not defenceless. Trust Tamar to find a way.

Of course, the Faerie queen had a lot more practise at using Faerie magic than Tamar had; he tensed up again.[*]

Overhead, Denny noticed a dragon was flying with single-minded determination in a straight line, head down and wings back as if it was in a tremendous hurry.

---

[*] Denny, by the way, was dead wrong here, on all counts.

'Dragons?' he thought idly. 'Well I never.'

But after it had flown away, making a sound like a demented buzz saw, he did not think much about it. For instance, he did not notice that the direction it was headed in was directly towards the Key Stones.

* * *

When Hecaté had surmised that the point of the changelings was infiltration, she was only half right.

In fact, there is a much more practical reason why Faeries do this. It is because they have to.

Everything has a balance in the universe, if you add something then you have to take something away and vice versa. Otherwise, the balance is thrown off.

Faeries cannot just enter the mortal world. They have to make space for themselves. They have to take something out. If they do not, they will be pulled back to the Faerie realm. Usually they take children, because it is easier.

But when a Faerie child is born into this world, it belongs here just like a mortal child would. New life is easier; the universe makes room for it.

So now, when a human child is taken to the Faerie realm it can be replaced with a Faerie child that was born in the mortal realm and still leave room for another Faerie to cross over, leaving the Faerie children to grow up among the humans, and no one the wiser.

Infiltration is just a bonus.

So, when Tamar and Denny went into the Faerie realm they left a gap behind in *this* world, a sucking void that was calling out to be filled, a void that was, weight for weight, about the capacity of a smallish dragon.

* * *

'I'm *sure* this will create a paradox,' complained Denny as they rode along. He just could not leave this alone; it had been preying on his mind. It may have had something to do with him having been trapped in a time paradox before. This sort of thing made him nervous

'If they – the other us-ess, are out there now doing the same things that we did before, then aren't we just going to keep ending up back here?' he added.

'That's right,' said Tamar cheerfully. 'But it isn't a paradox, it's a time loop. We've probably had this conversation before.'

'I don't remember it,'

'Well you won't. We'll never know the difference.'

'So we just keep going round and round in time forever? That's a *paradox*!'

'No. A paradox is when you don't *know* that you're going round and round forever. We can break the cycle anytime we like because we're outside of it.'

'Now would be a good time don't you think? Let's just …'

'No. I'm going after her. You don't have to come.'

'Look, how the hell do you know all this?'

Tamar stared at him as if he was daft. 'I know *everything*.' she said eventually.

Denny had forgotten this. He blinked. 'Everything?' he said. '*Really* everything?' this was a worrying thought.

'Everything I *want* to know, yes.'

Denny relaxed. There are some things a person does not *want* to know.

Tamar reined in the pony and jumped off.

'Look,' she said. 'When we get back to the point in time that we left from, we'll remember all this, we can remember the future now, can't we? It's not a paradox when you can do that. I'm not explaining this very well, but basically, we're *visiting* this time, we are not part of it (nice job by the way. You probably did it instinctively this way). And we can go home again, and everything will be the same, except one thing. I'm going to kill her.'

'And if you do that, it'll change things,' pointed out Denny.

'Not enough,' she said. 'It'll just save us the bother of doing it later.'

'You're crazy,' said Denny.

'No I'm not. Listen to me. The Faeries will still attack, Jack will still find the gauntlet and Cindy will still run away.

It's already *happened*. We can't change that unless we change what *they* do.' She meant the other versions of themselves.

Then what's the point?'

'We can stop *her*. This is the point in time when we can do it, when she's vulnerable. Can't you just accept that?'

'No, because if we stop her now, it *will* change things. The Faeries attacked under her command. If we stop her now ...' Denny stopped as his brain caught up with his ears. 'Oh!' he said.

'It's all already happened,' said Tamar gently.

'I see,' said Denny. 'Well, what are we waiting for?'

* * *

Back in the present or the future or whatever Jack Stiles was having problems of his own.

He had not told the others because they seemed nervous enough as it was, but the gauntlet was having a strange effect on him. At first, it seemed like a faint buzzing in his ears. Then it upgraded to a ringing, and now he was certain. He was hearing things. Faeries to be exact, every Faerie in the world, he could hear what they were thinking. It could be useful he realised, if he could only control it, separate out the sounds but all he was getting currently was a cacophony of thoughts and he could not shut it off.

It was like having the worst migraine in the world.

* * *

The Faerie queen was currently searching for Tamar, just as Tamar had been searching for her and with the same amount of success i.e. none at all.

What this came down to in the final analysis, was a catfight over a man. And the Faerie Queen intended to win it. She had never lost her man before.

Of course, Tamar's motives may have been a little more heroic, saving the world etc. But for the Queen of the Sidhe, it was all about getting what she wanted. She was petty and proud of it. She was a Faerie after all.

That was where Stiles was going wrong. The noise in his head was not the same as if he could hear the thoughts of *people*. They were just the janglings of a thousand empty minds. It was *all* background noise, and he would have done better to ignore it and concentrate on the one pure thought that streamed from every mind he was connected to. *Kill, Kill, Kill.*

The Queen could sense Tamar's power, and this, she believed, was the way to her mind, but suddenly she sat up and snapped her eyes open. '*What?*' she cried. 'Now *she's* gone too?'

* * *

'Will the others notice we're gone?' asked Denny suddenly

'Oh yes,' said Tamar. 'We're on a little trip, that's all.'

'I don't understand all this.' moaned Denny. 'I thought we could go back to the point where we left, and it would be like nothing happened.'

'That's right, but until we get back, we'll be gone ... look can I give you some advice?'

'Okay.'

'Don't try to understand it, just enjoy the ride.'

Denny huffed. '*Enjoy* it!'

'It helps if you think of things just happening one after another. We are here, and this is now.'

~ Chapter Twenty Three ~

CINDY WAS IN her room alone, having just put Jacky to sleep. She pulled her slip over her head and shook her hair out. A long hot bath sounded good. She was standing there completely naked, when her witch senses told her she was being watched.

She froze and looked surreptitiously around the room for something that could be used as a weapon. There was a conspicuous lack of hard or edged items in the room, which leaned toward the fluffy or at least feathery and downy elements of décor. The fact that she was naked was of secondary consideration to Cindy; after all, she had nothing to be ashamed of. Where most women would have grabbed a bathrobe, Cindy eventually lighted on a heavy looking jewellery box and headed towards the window with a determined look on her face.

The intruder, who had been watching her with appreciation for some time, realised that he had been discovered and backed away suddenly forgetting that he was on the third floor. He fell thirty feet with a loud yell and landed in the rose bushes with a scream.

All this noise might have attracted some attention, but there was only Stiles to hear it at the moment, and he had enough noises in his head to be going on with.

The infuriated Cindy lit over the balcony without stopping to think, landed lightly on the grass (still naked), and hauled her "visitor" roughly out of the rose patch.

'What the hell ...?' then she saw who it was and backed away rapidly. '*You?*'

Finvarra gave her a charming smile. 'My darling girl,' he said. 'It's been too long.'

Cindy suddenly became horribly aware that she was, in fact, naked. It may have been the way he was looking at her – as if she was a particularly appetising pastry. Unable to manifest without a long chant and certain ingredients, she decided to become invisible instead.

'I can still see you,' said Finvarra amusedly. 'I think it's only fair to tell you.'

Cindy did not believe him, and her face must have said as much because he added. 'And you can take that look off your face, I *can* see you, I exist in both worlds remember?' *

'Don't be silly,' said Cindy far more bravely than she felt. 'How could I possibly remember anything about you, I don't even know you.'

'Oh yes you do,' he told her. 'You've just forgotten.'

* * *

Night fell suddenly over the Faerie realm. And I do mean suddenly. It was like a light abruptly going out in a room with no windows. Not a scrap of light was left, not a glimmer. It was eerie.

Denny did not like this development, even though he had excellent night vision this depended on there being at least a *little* ambient light and there really was none at all.

'Wait,' said Tamar. A few seconds later, an overlarge moon popped into the sky like a searchlight coming on. There were

---

* Becoming invisible, for a witch at least, is simply a matter of letting yourself drift onto the astral plane where ordinary people cannot see you.]

no stars, but Denny had a feeling that it was only a matter of time before they too were "switched on"

'How do you do that?' he asked her genuinely impressed. 'How did you know, I mean?'

'You just have to think – crooked,' she said dismissively. 'I'm good at that.'

'Ain't that the truth,' muttered Denny.

'This place isn't real,' she carried on as if he had said nothing, she was used to his acerbic little asides. 'It's been cobbled together using ideas of what *is* real, but it's not quite *right*. The moon comes up at night, therefore – voila.' She indicated the moon in the sky. 'There's a moon. The fact that it looks more like a TV spotlight is neither here nor there. At least not to us.'

'Askphrit did better in the deleted file,' said Denny. 'At least it *looked* real in there.

'I think I've worked out why the Dwarfs hate the Faeries so much,' said Tamar suddenly.'

'What? Why?'

'Look around you,' said Tamar. 'It's *fairyland*. I mean, how are dwarfs perceived nowadays? Fairy tale creatures, the Faeries did that to them. They created an entire mythology based on *this*.' she waved a hand disparagingly. 'Ugh,' she added. 'Hi-ho, indeed,'

'Not just them,' said Denny gloomily. 'The centaurs and fauns and everything too.'

'So what do we do now – boss?' he added after a pause.

'I don't know,' she admitted. 'There still isn't really enough light to see by … maybe …'

'There!' shouted Denny suddenly and pointed to a region of the sky that was lighting up in sections to fill in the shape of the Faerie castle.

'Ah,' said Tamar, 'a trap.'

'Oh definitely,' agreed Denny. 'She might as well have just hung a large neon sign in the sky with an arrow pointing towards her.'

'Yes, it could say, "Don't Go Near the Castle".'

They both laughed.

'Well, said Denny. 'Since we *know* it's a trap …?'

'Yeah, since we know that, if we go now she'll have us right where we want her. Let's wait until morning. Let her sweat a bit. Wonder what we're up to. She'll be nice and jittery then when we *do* get there.'

'She could escape in the dark,' pointed out Denny.

'She won't. She'll be waiting for us. I *know* it. This is between me and her now. It's got to be finished.'

'What are you going to do? Apart from kill her I mean, I mean *how*?'

Tamar looked puzzled. 'How?' she repeated.

'Yeah,' he counted off on his fingers. 'No magic, no iron, no music …'

'Maybe I'll strangle her,' said Tamar with an enigmatic look.

Denny took this to mean that she had not actually got as far as planning the "how" of this operation. However, he was not too worried. They often worked like this, off the cuff as it were. Sometimes, plans just got in the way. Something usually came up, and no one was better at improvising mayhem than Tamar.

If she had not been an evil megalomaniac, Denny could have felt sorry for the Faerie Queen. She had no idea what was about to happen to her. The fact that Tamar, as yet, had no idea either was a mere detail.

He was completely wrong about this as it happened. Tamar *did* have a plan. She just did not want to tell him, in case it did not work.

They settled down, on a bank of mossy grass under the luminous moon to wait until morning.

* * *

'Why don't we go for dinner?' said Finvarra, hopefully holding out an exquisite dress. Cindy looked at it in distaste.

'Please?' he said. 'We have a lot to talk about.'

'So talk,' said Cindy without offering to move.

'We can bring the boy with us, if that would make you more comfortable,' he said, 'although if I had wanted to take him from you, I could have done it before.'

'Maybe you wouldn't have wanted me to know it was you,' she countered weakly. This was, at best, a spurious argument and Cindy knew it, but she was in no mood to make things easy for him.

Finvarra just stared at her, a mute plea in his eyes. Eventually she muttered. 'Oh all *right* then,' and took the dress ungraciously.

'I want to go to Annabel's,' she told him. 'And you're paying.'

Finvarra nodded. 'As you wish,' he said. 'Do you want a limousine?'

It took Cindy a few moments to realise that this last was not, in fact, a piece of sarcasm at her expense.

She shook her head. 'I want to go on that,' she said pointing mischievously at Denny's muddy, scratched up motorbike. And was immensely gratified to see the horror materialize on Finvarra's face.

'You'll spoil your pretty dress,' he said.

'And ruin my hair,' agreed Cindy. She was enjoying this. This must be how Denny felt all the time. He seemed to enjoy his "take me or leave me" attitude. As far as Cindy was concerned, she would not be a "trophy date" for this – person. She had no intention of letting him think that just because he was handsome and charming, that she was going to make *any* effort for him at all. That would seem as if she were – *grateful* or something. And she was not – not at all. If he wanted a piece of arm candy to show off, he was going to be disappointed. She might have been talked into going along with it, but she was not going to let him have it all his own way.

'I'll let you drive,' she said with the air of one conferring a great favour.

Finvarra did not look as if he greatly appreciated it.

But he bowed graciously. 'As you wish,' he said to her complete surprise.

'Wait a minute,' she said, and roughly ripped the dress up both seams right up to the thigh. Finvarra's eyes widened.

'Can't sit on a motorbike in a tight skirt,' she said playfully. 'Okay, I'm ready.'

Finvarra hesitated.

'We don't have to go,' she said. 'I don't care, you can just bugger off if you like. Or you can put up with me as I am,' she grinned, she was flying now. 'Take me or leave me,' she told him.

'As you are,' said Finvarra apparently coming to some internal decision. He climbed onto the motorbike and held out a hand courteously to help her on, just as he would have, had it been the proposed limousine.

'That's better,' said Cindy hiding her confusion admirably.

They entered the restaurant with Finvarra holding her arm proudly, just as if she had been properly dressed, and they marched in as if completely oblivious of the stares and muttering of the other patrons.

'Shabby chic,' said Cindy blithely in a loud voice. 'It's the latest thing.' She looked like she had been through a hurricane; she had bits of twig in her hair.

She had to admit she was impressed, despite herself, at the way Finvarra dealt with it; he could not have been ready for this. Cindy was vain, everybody knew it, the idea that she would go out in public looking like a tattered urchin with no makeup on and no shoes even (her feet were filthy) was inconceivable. And yet Finvarra handled it with gracious aplomb and treated her like a duchess all evening.

They were at the end of the second course, and he still had not got to the point. Cindy's curiosity was almost at bursting point, but she was too well drilled in the peculiar etiquette of this sort of situation to point this out. *He* had invited *her*; therefore, it was for him to bring up the reason in his own good time. Besides, she had no intention of letting him know that she was curious, or interested even. *She* was doing *him* a favour. That was the fiction here, and her pride demanded that she maintain the façade.

'I expect you're wondering why I asked you here?' he said suddenly as the supercilious waiter left with their empty plates and his nose in the air.

'Well it wasn't to show me off anyway,' laughed Cindy glancing at the waiter.

'You look beautiful,' he said with apparent sincerity. 'You always do,'

Despite herself, Cindy's pulse quickened. This sounded like the beginning of one of those adventures that had been so plentiful in her past. It was an age and a half since she had been wined and dined and flattered like this. She felt better than she had for a long, long time. And after all, why not? He *was* handsome and charming and almost certainly experienced and no doubt skilled

He was certainly good at the compliments, and if he was the enemy, well she was forewarned about that. No doubt she would learn far more from him than he would from her.

Finvarra sighed. 'Where to begin,' he said. 'I have such a lot to tell you.'

'Begin at the beginning,' said Cindy. 'I usually find that's best.'

'That was a very long time ago,' he said. 'A thousand years.'

'I'm not that bloody old,' said Cindy indignantly.

'I am,' he said. 'And *you* may not be, but nevertheless, our story does begin that far back.'

He leaned across the table and took her hand. 'You may have a young body my dear, but you have a very old soul.'

He leaned back. 'I have been searching for you for a thousand years. I'm only sorry that she came back and found you first. It has caused so much trouble.'

'You will kindly explain what you are talking about,' said Cindy with the forced politeness of someone hanging on to the last shreds of their patience.

'I'm sorry if I sound cryptic,' he sighed again. 'I was hoping that you would remember. But that, it seems, was too much to hope for.'

'Remember *what*?

'How much I once loved you.' He leaned in close and held her gaze in a hypnotic stare. 'And still do,' he said.

Cindy started to shake.

* * *

Stiles was shaking too. In his case, it was because he was dying for a drink. The voices in his head were driving him mad and he kept setting the furniture on fire by accident.

Learning to use your new super powers was not as easy as Denny had made it look. Of course, Denny had always been laid back about everything, whereas Stiles was pretty tightly wound at the best of times, and now was not the best of times, what with the thoughts of a million Faeries roaming haphazardly through his mind. And, of course, at the time Denny had been singularly unhampered by moral considerations whereas Stiles was worried about hurting people. No wonder it had been easier for him.

Hecaté decided it was time to do something about the situation. She had left him alone in the hope that he would come to her – but it had apparently not occurred to him to seek the advice of the only other deity within his personal circle.

'And he calls himself a policeman,' she thought. 'Hah!' More importantly, he had not thought to go to his wife and confide in her. But that was mortal men for you – immortal men too if she remembered rightly.

She eschewed the small talk and got straight to the point, a trick learned directly from him. You cannot live with a policeman and not learn a thing or two about interrogation. First rule, you already know whatever it is they are not telling you. Assume that and let them fill in the blanks in an attempt to keep up.

'You can hear them all can you not?' she said without preliminaries. 'In your head. I imagine it is difficult for a human to manage. I am used to it of course.'

Stiles stirred and gave her a good view of his blurred and bloodshot eyes. 'You?' he said.' 'You can hear …?'

'Every witch in the world, yes.'

Stiles sat up interestedly. 'Really? How do you stand it?'

'It has always been that way,' she told him. 'It is part of being a god. But I can help you.'

'Can you help me shut it off?'

'Is that what you really want?'

Stiles thought about it. 'No, not really, but I don't think I can take much more of it without going insane.'

'A human mind was never meant to deal with this power,' mused Hecaté. 'But then, not *all* of your mind is human any more. Part of it is the deity now. He's in there with you, is he not?'

The gauntlet …' said Stiles vaguely. 'He runs it from inside my head, only … it's me too. But it's him that tells me how.'

'So he is in there? That is the part of you that can hear the Faeries. Let him deal with it.'

Stiles frowned. 'It's that easy?' he said. 'Just … let him deal with it. But he's *me*. I don't see …'

'Just try it. Separate your mind.'

Stiles closed his eyes. After a minute, he smiled and began to snore.

Hecaté smiled. 'I knew you could do it,' she said softly and leaned down to kiss his forehead. 'Sleep well my love, sweet dreams.'

* * *

The morning hit them like a hammer. The sun did not so much rise as shoot up into the sky like a rocket and burst into flame.

'Bloody hell!' said Denny but more as a matter of form than anything else, they had been expecting something like this.

Tamar laughed; it had been a long time since he had seen her so happy. It was the prospect of violence ahead. Denny had always deplored this side of her nature, but he had to admit she reined it in most of the time. Only those who deserved it felt her wrath. And no one could argue that Queen Onagh did not deserve it.

He brushed his hair away from his face and rubbed his gritty eyes, he could do with a wash. And, naturally, there was a handy stream nearby.

The water was so blue it looked dyed, and so still that it reflected a perfect mirror image of his face.

'Ugh,' he said and bent down to splash said face with (hopefully) cold water.

It happened so fast that even Tamar could not react in time. A figure, that appeared to be composed of water, itself rose vertically from the stream's surface, extended watery arms, grabbed Denny round the neck and pulled him in.

There was not even a splash. He just disappeared.

Tamar forced herself to remain calm. She glanced from a safe distance into the water, but it had regained its smooth mirror-like surface. There was nothing to be seen.

'Big mistake Onagh,' she muttered. 'If you want a fight, you'll get more than you bargained for. Denny's mine and no one's taking him away from me. I *know* you can hear me! I'm coming to get you.'

'Be afraid,' she thought dramatically. 'Be very afraid.'

She raised her head and shouted to the blazing pink sky. 'I'M COMING TO GET YOU!'

* * *

'Here we go again,' thought Denny wearily. It was even the same dungeon – or an exact facsimile anyway.

There were differences this time though. No Athame taunting him from a safe distance for one thing (he had not brought it with him). No other Faeries had appeared yet either. It would appear that there would be no torture this time.

She was different this time too. Softer, gentler, more conciliatory, and, if it had not been too incredible, she seemed almost humble.

'No singing here,' she said. 'No breath.'

Denny nodded. He knew it, he and Tamar, and now he and the Queen had not actually been speaking to each other in the usual way at all, he realised. He was so used to telepathy that he had not really noticed it until now. Even now, he barely noticed the difference.

'No magic, at least no magic that *you* can use,' she shrugged. 'Unless you join me.'

Denny contrived by his expression to indicate that this was not even worth answering.

She pouted. 'Look at me!' she ordered him petulantly. 'I shouldn't have to beg you to love me.'

'I shouldn't bother if I were you,' he said callously.

Her face darkened. 'So you say,' she said. 'But I have broken stronger men than you.'

'Uh oh,' he thought. 'Looks like the torture might be back on the menu after all.'

She smiled. 'We are in *my* world now,' she said. 'New rules.' She brought her face up close to his. 'Tell me you love me,' she ordered.

Denny opened his mouth to say it. Then shut it again firmly. *'No! Don't say it, but I want to. No you don't. It hurts. Shut up. don't say it. Don't say it!'*

'You can bugger off,' he managed. 'I'm not that easy to manipulate.'

She spun on her heel and stalked out of the dungeon.

Denny sagged; this was not going to be easy.

* * *

Cindy lay on her bed staring at the ceiling. She was in shock, incredulous and yet she believed him. She had seen the love in his eyes; it went fathoms deep.

Apparently, a thousand years before, Finvarra had met and fell in love with a witch. Her name had been Alisande and she was apparently an ancestor, in direct line, of Cindy herself. But there was more to it than that.

Cindy had heard the legends about the witches of the olden days passing on their souls to their descendants. A measure of immortality, the only one available to witches, who were basically human, but she had never believed it – until now.

Alisande had given her life to seal the portal and trap the Faerie Queen. Cindy knew this was true. What she had experienced in her unconscious state on the motorway had not been a premonition; it had been a memory.

That it had become inextricably mixed up with her present life was not so surprising, given that it come to her as a dream. The feelings she had felt as Alisande for Finvarra had translated into her current feelings for Denny. Or had they? What *did* she feel? And for whom?

What *was* certain was that Alisande had made her tragic sacrifice for the same reasons as she, Cindy, had done in her dream. Queen Onagh had been horrendously jealous over Finvarra. She would never have let him go. She would have died rather. So Alisande had killed herself for his sake. And the Queen had now set her sights on Denny instead. Could that explain Cindy's confusion? Was she just reacting to a thousand year old memory, or were her feelings for Denny real and unrelated?

Finvarra had told her that, before she died, Alisande had told him she would be reborn in the body of a descendant. And the Queen had heard her. It had, no doubt, he said, seemed fitting to Onagh that she find this prophesied descendant to seal the stones once more. Both the soul *and* the blood of the same witch. It had a nice mythic ring to it. Faeries *like* mythic.

Coming across Denny had been a mere bonus. She had been *looking*, as Finvarra had, for Cindy.

And Jacky? It was just as he said. Finvarra had sent Jacky to watch over her in his absence. There was something he was not telling her here; she knew it. Something about Jacky or perhaps her own son. But she had not pushed for more. She had enough to deal with for the moment.

Then there was the problem of Finvarra's expectations. It seemed that he still loved ... no *adored* her. Alisande had apparently captivated the Faerie King in a quite unexpected and wholly irreversible manner. And he had clearly expected that, when he found her, the relationship would just pick up where it had so abruptly left off.

He had made it quite clear that he fully expected her to return his feelings. But a thousand years is a long time. He may not have forgotten, but *she* had.

Cindy's heart, for whatever reason, now belonged to someone else.

Just as Denny's did, the pragmatist inside told her.

What a mess.

Even as she wrestled with herself, she knew that she would take him. Better to be loved than be in love. Being in love hurt, but being loved had no real disadvantages and Finvarra's adoration would provide balm to her wounded heart. Besides, she had a feeling that, if rejected, Finvarra was capable of being just as vindictive as his estranged wife. This was not something Cindy wanted to provoke.

There was a crash and some loud cursing from downstairs. Jack was setting fire to things again.

Cindy turned over on to her side and sighed. 'And the fun never stops around here,' she thought.

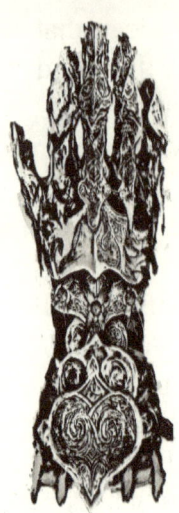

~ Chapter Twenty Four ~

DENNY TRIED TO concentrate on Tamar's face as the Queen tried her best to make him forget it. It was a battle of wills and the Queen was winning.

She held all the cards, and she knew it. She even knew, and Denny was at a loss to explain this (until he realised that she was looking into his mind) that they had come back in time for her.

'I'm flattered,' she had sneered. 'Now, *who* do you love?'

'Tamar,' said Denny dully, as if the word had no meaning for him anymore but was simply a repetition of a long forgotten idea.

The Faerie Queen smiled. This was getting better, if only he would let go. She really did not want to hurt him like this. Well, all right, she had no real problem with hurting him as such, but it would have been better for her pride if she had not been forced into this.

She looked at his face, all strained and pale and said gently. 'It doesn't have to be this way, just let go of her, let go of your stubbornness. Tell me you love me.'

'He never will,' came a voice from behind her.

The Faerie Queen turned and snarled viscously.

'He's mine,' Tamar snarled back.

'I'll *never* give him up,' hissed the Queen. 'I'll die before I give him to *you*.'

'I think,' said Denny weakly, 'that that just means that you both have the same aim in mind.'

The Faerie Queen was disconcerted. Tamar was just standing there – smiling. It was unnerving; even Denny was unsure – and he *knew* her.

'You can't win,' the Faerie Queen tried.

Tamar just stood there smiling serenely.

'I have all the power here.'

More smiling.

'I can wipe you out with a single thought,'

Tamar stood as still as a statue. The smile on her face seemed fixed forever.

'Don't think I won't do it.' the Queen looked uncertainly at Denny who shrugged – a difficult feat when handcuffed to a pillar.

'Stop *smiling*, this isn't funny.'

The smile widened. And Tamar spoke at last. 'I've already won,' she said.

Denny opened his eyes wide. Either there was something that she had not told him, or this was a monstrous piece of bluff. Either way, it boded ill for the Queen. When Tamar bluffed, she usually did it with a stacked deck.

'Look at you,' Tamar sneered. 'You can't even get one wretched mortal (no offence darling) to say he loves you. You have no power here, or anywhere else, over *us*, go ahead do your worst. I'm asking you.'

'What are you up to?' wondered the Queen aloud.

'Up to? I'm not up to *any*thing. I never am.'

'She never is,' confirmed Denny obediently.

'What *is* she up to?' he wondered in the privacy of his own head (or so he thought).

'I heard that,' said the Queen.

'Damn,' thought Denny. 'I forgot you were in here too.'

But Tamar had not forgotten.

It was all part of her plan.

* * *

Stiles was listening to the news with a despondent air. It was not the normal news (all normal media communications had been suspended under the tyrannical regime of the Faeries) but a pirate radio broadcast put together by a band of rebel humans. The news was depressing. But at least it was not Faerie propaganda.

It had got beyond their control now; it was all too big. There were concentration camps according to the pirate radio jocks (although that might just be scaremongering, anti-propaganda they called it didn't they?)

Stiles had an uncanny sensation that he was actually in one of those Sci-Fi movies where frighteningly advanced aliens take over the planet. The only difference was that the Faeries were not actually eating people – as far as he knew. In those movies, the hero always finds the alien's weakness and exploits it, therefore, saving the world to general rejoicing.

Well, this was not a movie and Stiles was not a hero. He was past forty and got out of breath running too fast up the stairs. Or he had until recently. No, Stiles was just a copper (retired) and coppers arrested people, they did not save the world, at least, not by themselves. What he needed was Denny and Tamar. That was how it worked. He found the crime, and they kicked the criminal's butt. He did not know where they were now, but he just had to hope that, wherever they were, that was what they were doing.

He listened with half an ear to the rantings of the rebels on the radio. Secret rebel forces, anti-propaganda, fear and defiance. The sounds of a world under siege.

He switched it off; it was not as if they could tell him anything that he did not already know.

He glanced around the room and spotted something familiar. Not familiar to him exactly, but familiar to Leir.

Now he just had to figure out what the hell it was.

* * *

Cindy came into the main hall; she had taken Jacky to his nursery for a nap and wanted someone to talk to. She found Stiles.

'Oh,' she said in surprise. 'You fixed my lamp. I thought it had been thrown out.'

'Lamp?' said Stiles. 'Is that what it is?'

Cindy settled into an armchair and took it from him. 'Yes, it's a very old oil lamp,' she said, 'sort of a family heirloom.'

'I thought you'd bought it,' said Stiles.

'Why would I buy something this ugly?' laughed Cindy.

'It *is* horrible,' agreed Stiles. 'Is it worth much?'

'Practically priceless, according to my mother.'

Stiles held out a hand. 'May I?'

She handed it back to him.

Stiles stared at it intently, and Cindy shifted in her chair. 'There's something I …' she began.

'This isn't a lamp,' stated Stiles abruptly.'

'No?' said Cindy disinterestedly.

'No,' he said excitedly. 'This is what we've been looking for. This is how we defeat the Faeries.'

Cindy looked sceptical. 'What,' she said, 'with my old lamp?'

* * *

The Faerie Queen hesitated, and Tamar struck. It was a powerful mental blow and the Queen actually staggered backwards.

'Y-You can't do that,' she gasped as she regained her breath.

'Anything you can do, I can do better,' said Tamar tauntingly. 'Don't look at *him*,' she ordered as the Faerie Queen turned uncertainly again to Denny. 'He's not going to help you. He's with me. You have no friends here.'

But the Faerie Queen, like all her kind, had no idea of friendship. The closest they can get to the idea is an enemy that you have not killed yet. Under these rules, Denny qualified. Therefore, she turned to him beseechingly.

'No magic here,' said Tamar, 'except yours. Look at *me*.'

The Faerie Queen found her gaze dragged unwillingly back to Tamar who watched her like a cat watching a mouse. Then she hit her again.

The Faerie Queen sank to her knees. 'So you might wonder how I am doing this?' said Tamar. 'How I even got in here against your will.' She laughed cruelly. 'Keep wondering.'

'She's using the Faerie magic,' thought Denny and immediately regretted it.

But the Faerie Queen gave no sign that she had noticed.

Instead, she struck back. It was the last mistake she ever made.

* * *

'What are we going to do with it then, bash them over the head with it?' Cindy examined the lamp critically. It just looked like a lamp to her. The wick was missing

'Cindy, where did your family get this?' said Stiles urgently.

'I don't know,'

'I gave it to you – your ancestor rather,' said Finvarra appearing in the room. 'He bowed courteously to Stiles. 'Leir,' he said.

'Finvarra,' replied Stiles automatically. 'One of the faithful, I seem to – to … remember?' he finished uncertainly.

'You gave it away?' he said suddenly as if someone else was speaking through him. 'I did not know that?' he added thoughtfully.

'What's going on?' he added aggressively – as Stiles, and he looked suspiciously from one to the other.

Cindy and Finvarra looked at one another. 'It's a long story,' said Cindy.

'It is a strange thing to be faced with One's god in these circumstances,' said Finvarra grinning nervously.

Cindy nodded. 'Tell me about it,' she said.

'You get used to it,' she added as Hecaté entered the room to see what was going on.

*

It was later.

Stories had been told, explanations made. And now an awkward silence reigned.

Stiles coughed and everyone jumped. 'Well,' he said. 'Well, er … moving on. Finvarra, since you now seem to be a part of this, that is to say …'

'Tell us about the lamp,' said Cindy. 'Why did you give it to … er … Alisande? What is it?'

Finvarra nodded towards Stiles. 'He knows,' he said.

'It is a trap,' said Stiles as three pairs of eyes focussed on him. 'And we thought it had been lost forever.'

'We?' thought Cindy. 'Oh blimey!'

'It might as well have been,' said Finvarra, 'as far as we were concerned, since only you can use it.'

'Yes, we built it long ago in accordance with an old arrangement. It was not a trap then, but rather a transportation device.'

Stiles focussed and became one person again – himself. 'Look, he said. 'I think I should begin from the beginning, as it were.' He looked mockingly at them.

'You lot don't know the half of it,' he said. He looked at Finvarra. 'Not even you,' he added. 'You don't even know who you really are.'

* * *

When the Faerie Queen struck out at Tamar with all her mind, Tamar reacted in a way that no one could have predicted. She did nothing.

She did not have to.

The Queen had been labouring, thanks to Denny's errant thoughts, under the impression that Tamar was using Faerie magic. She was not. She just wanted the Queen to *think* she was.

The Queen lashed out viciously and terminally at the source of the Faerie magic that was attacking her. She died instantly.

A better way to go, as Tamar dryly observed, than she deserved.

'I warned her,' said Tamar undoing Denny's shackles. 'No one could say I didn't warn her. I said, clear as a bell, there was no magic here but hers, but would she listen?'

'She was fighting herself?' said Denny.

'Oh, yes, I just … helped her along.'

'Goaded her you mean?'

'Well?'

'But you hit her with a mind blow, I saw you. I *felt* it?'

Tamar raised her eyebrows. 'Did I?' she said. 'Or did she just *think* I did?'

'You did.'

'No, I didn't. I wouldn't know how. But she was expecting me to, so she hit out first and only hit herself. She was a bit confused I expect.'

Tamar tapped her head expressively. 'Psychology,' she said enigmatically. 'You have to understand your enemy. Now she didn't understand me at all, she couldn't imagine that I would come in here with nothing, it's certainly not the sort of thing she would do herself.'

'That's true,' muttered Denny.

'All I had to do was make her edgy, get her worried. She did the rest.'

'It was risky, though.'

'Well, yes, a bit. But I had nothing else. No magic here.'

'Except hers.'

'Yes, how do you think I got in here? She was expecting me, that's how. She knew I was coming and, since she thought I could get in anyway, she just let me in. Faerie magic, it's all about messing with your head.'

'She didn't stand a chance against you then,' said Denny.

'That's right,' said Tamar smugly. 'It's not about what's real,' she said. 'Not here, it's about what you believe. And she believed that I had the power of the Faerie magic.

'Even though you didn't.'

'I had the power that she gave me by her belief. She believed it because *you* believed it and she was messing around in your head, but that's all I needed.'

'You *knew* that I believed it?'

'I made sure you did,' she said.

She took one last look behind her as they prepared to leave and clapped her hands. 'I *don't* believe in faeries,' she said triumphantly.

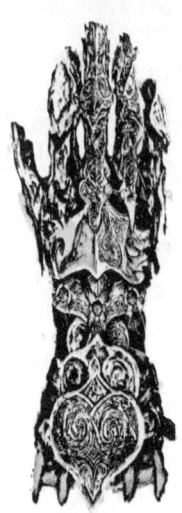

~ Chapter Twenty Five ~

'A VERY LONG time ago, in a galaxy very far away. ™'

'SIDHE WARS!'

'Jack stop being a prat,' said Cindy, 'and get to the point.

'What, it's okay when Denny does it?' said Stiles indignantly.

'I think, my dear,' said Hecaté soothingly as Cindy went red. 'That we are all just very anxious to know what you have to tell us.'

'I was about to,' said Stiles. 'When she …'

'*Now*, Jack,' said Hecaté in a wifely warning manner.

'Oh all right,' said Stiles reluctantly giving up his dramatic moment.

He needn't have worried. What he told them knocked them sideways. Even, as he had predicted, Finvarra.

'Basically then,' he said. 'It's like this. 'The Tuatha De Danann, from whom all the Sidhe are descended, came here from another planet many millennia ago to escape a horrible war. The Sidhe are aliens, they just don't remember it.'

Having thrown his bombshell, he sat back, amused at their stunned faces.

Then the arguing began.

* * *

The Faerie world was vanishing. Behind them, the castle crumbled like month old wedding cake. Very like it actually, the castle had had a distinctly wedding-cake look about it to begin with. And as they looked up ...

'Oh *no*,' shouted Denny. 'The *sky* is falling.'

It was – literally.

All around them, the Faerie realm was fading away leaving in its place a vast howling wilderness.

'It's her,' shouted Denny above the thundering wind. 'She was what held this place together. And now she's gone ...'

Tamar stopped running. 'No,' she realised, 'this is just another "Dontgonearthecastle". It's just meant to scare us.'

Time to stop and *think*.

Denny skidded to a halt. 'What are you doing?' he yelled. 'We have to get out of here.'

'Why?'

'Why? *Why*? Because the place is coming down around our ears. That is traditionally the time when you *leave*! Preferably as fast as you can, and ... Why the hell am I explaining this to you? We don't have *time* for this. Come *on*!' and he tried to drag her with him. He might as well have tried to drag her from a black hole, a phenomenon that the Faerie world was increasingly resembling.

Here and there the remnants of the Faerie's bright world could still be seen, but it was full of holes through which could be seen – nothing. Vast swathes of nothing as far as the eye could see. It was blue.

'Wait,' said Tamar.

They waited; there really was no arguing with Tamar in this mood. In any mood really, if he was honest, but he still tried.

The wind slowed, the howling decreased to a dull roar. 'Don't buy into it,' said Tamar. 'It's not real, remember?'

Then suddenly, as if it was giving up, the whole world went dark. There was a smell of damp earth.

A faint greenish light filtered through from above them; the air was cool, water trickled in the distance.

'We're underground,' said Denny in surprise.

'And the Sidhe fled underground,' quoted Tamar inaccurately. 'We should have known.'

'Well, let's get out of here,' said Denny.

'No, let's find whatever it was that this elaborate illusion was set up to hide,' said Tamar. '*Then* we'll get out of here.'

'You don't know that it was set up to hide something,' said Denny reasonably.

'I do,' she said shortly.

'She might not have set it up to hide anything,' he repeated hopelessly. (Sometimes he tried to argue even, no *especially*, when there was no point.)

'*I* would have,' said Tamar.

'Oh right.' There really was no arguing with this logic.

'What are we looking for then?'

'Whatever she didn't want us to find.'

'What's that then?'

Tamar glared at him. 'Are you doing this on purpose?' she said.

'Just admit it,' he said. 'You have no idea, have you?'

'I'll know it when I see it,' she said mulishly.

'See what?'

'Shut up.'

* * *

The argument came to an abrupt end when Stiles said in a loud, booming voice that he had never used before. 'The Faerie Queen is Dead,' and added in his normal voice when he had their attention. 'It's almost time.' He also added as if to himself. 'I *knew* she could do it.'

'Time for what?' asked Cindy, who was used to being in the dark about events and always asked. Cindy was invaluable to the group in this respect as it was often a relief to others who wanted to know but did not like to admit that they did not already know. Tamar was particularly guilty of this.

Three pairs of expectant eyes bored into Stiles.

He held up the lamp. 'This' he said. 'She can't protect them anymore. Tamar has killed her. It was all we were waiting for. Now we strike.'

This was news to the rest of them. 'We *were*?' said Cindy. 'No one told me. I didn't know we were waiting for anything in particular.'

Strike how?' asked Hecaté.

'What *I* want to know, begging your pardon my lord, is how you know she is dead indeed?' said Finvarra.

Stiles took the last question first. 'I feel their confusion,' he said, 'in my head. *They* know it, a strong influence has been removed, and they are in disarray, frightened. Would not your own subjects feel the same if *you* were to die?'

'No, they are self-reliant. I do not crave such power. But … they *would* know,' he conceded.

Stiles nodded and turned to Hecaté. 'We strike,' he said, 'by trapping them in the lamp. They have no defence against it now. Only the will of the Queen held them back from the fulfilment of the Oath.'

'Oath?' said two voices.

Only Finvarra nodded to himself.

'I was not here when the Oath was made,' said Stiles (as Leir). 'Finvarra knows more about the details I expect.'

'I made no Oath,' said Finvarra. 'All I know is that she made a deal with someone – a human I think – to keep her subjects safe when the slaughter began. But she broke her part of the bargain, which was to be expected. The lamp, I think was originally designed as a safe haven for her people. The human transported them inside it to a prepared sanctuary under the stones, if she promised never to trouble the mortal world again. But within the year she was back, and the lamp was mysteriously lost. That's all I know.'

'Why would he do all that?' asked Cindy, 'If the Faeries were being killed anyway?'

'Who knows why people do things?' said Finvarra. 'She probably promised him power or something.'

'She did,' said Stiles. 'He turned menacingly to Finvarra. 'You are not telling the whole story. But I can see into your mind. I have it now.'

He smiled at Cindy. 'A good question,' he said. 'And you shall have an answer. The Queen promised this man the power of the Faeries. He didn't use the lamp out of the goodness of his heart. He did it to trap the Faeries like a genie in a bottle. All the power of the Faeries at his command, but the Faerie Queen tricked him, and I must say, in this particular case, I do not blame her. *She* made the lamp, as a part of the deal. *He* had no such power. In return, he would take them to safety until the war between the humans and the Sidhe was concluded. But she knew he would not let them go. Indeed, she had bargained their freedom for their lives.'

'But she had no intention of giving up her freedom?' put in Cindy, who was keeping up admirably with this convoluted tale.

'So,' said Hecaté, summing up, 'the Queen built the lamp to hide her clan from the humans and made a deal with a greedy human that, if he would take the lamp and deliver it safely, he could come and claim it later and use the power of the Faeries inside for himself?'

'That's what I just said,' said Stiles impatiently

'I was just checking that I was following you correctly,' said Hecaté.

'What went wrong?' asked Cindy. Something kicked her brain for her attention. Finvarra was looking … sceptical? Puzzled?

'Quite simply, he should never have let her out,' said Stiles. 'She killed him.'

'And hid the lamp?' said Cindy. Something about the lamp, something Leir had said. What *was* it?

Finvarra laughed suddenly. 'She gave it to *me*, the fool,' he said.

'Why didn't you ever use it?' she asked him curiously.

'I told you, I can't. Besides, even if I could, it's not that simple. There would be … consequences. She has seen to that.'

Whatever it was, it was now screaming for Cindy's attention. Something did not *fit*. Something Leir had said earlier…

'When the lamp is lighted, all the Faeries under the oath, at least the Faeries within a certain range, will be drawn inside and cannot escape from within, unless the lamp is lighted again,' said Stiles. He was determined to get this in at any cost and nobody had asked, to his chagrin.

'Thousands of Faeries inside this small lamp?' said Cindy looking dubiously at it. 'How did she do that?'

'It's all relative,' said Stiles. 'After all she managed to create an entire realm inside a rather small underground cave.'

'How wide a range?' asked Hecaté.

'Don't worry about that,' said Stiles. 'We'll get them all. Now that she's not here to stop us.

'How could she have stopped us?' asked Cindy.

'Well, because she has been substituting human children for Faerie children for a long time now, most of the Faeries here *belong* here in this world. To remove them would create a vacuum, we couldn't do it without serious consequences, as Finvarra has said. But soon, because of what Tamar has done, that won't be a problem anymore.'

* * *

'Here!' shouted Tamar. 'You'll never guess what I've found.'

Denny came to look. There in the back of the cave, where they had been hidden from the world by the illusion of the Faerie realm were rows upon rows of sleeping children.

'Jackpot!' said Tamar.

* * *

'Won't the Faeries just be sucked back into the Faerie realm anyway, when Tamar brings the children back?' asked Cindy with commendable acuity. This was unnerving Stiles; Cindy was not supposed to be this quick.

'Not all of them,' said Stiles. 'Some of them were born here. In any case, there no longer *is* a Faerie realm. Tamar has destroyed it. It was never much more than an illusion anyway.'

Cindy picked up her lamp. 'You know this thing hasn't got a wick?' she said. 'How are we supposed to light it?'

The thought in Cindy's head finally lit a torch and waved it at her. 'Wait a minute,' she said. 'I thought you said that *you* had built the lamp.'

Stiles hesitated. 'Yes,' he said eventually. 'I did say that, didn't I?'

'She couldn't have made it on her own,' said Finvarra shrewdly. 'I *thought* it was odd. You helped her, didn't you? *You* made it for her,' he theorised, 'if she promised to behave herself in future?'

'Oh, all right then, yes, yes I did. She tricked me too. I, fool that I was, *believed* her. Her power over the mind is quite remarkable.' He sighed. 'The oath she took was to *me*, that is, the avatar at the time. *He* wanted the power of the faeries (an unworthy avatar and no doubt the reason why the plan failed) and I, from within, just wanted her … restrained. She broke the oath as soon as she became free.' He sighed. 'I no longer had the power to enforce the oath, and she knew it, she knew it when she made the oath. But I didn't realise that she knew it. She fooled me. And the lamp was gone. Forever, I thought.'

'And is that the *truth* this time?' said Cindy sternly.

Stiles was prevented from answering this question by the sudden and unexpected advent of an extremely infuriated dragon bursting through the windows and landing with a clatter on the tiles where it lay flapping it's wings feebly and gasping for breath. No one moved.

* * *

There were thousands of them, and it was obvious that many of them had been here for many years, even though they had not grown any older in that time. This was a problem indeed.

Tamar concentrated. This was going to be difficult even for her. To return these children not only to their place in the world, but also to their place in time.

'I need your help,' she admitted to Denny.

And even with the best intentions, it was surely not going to be possible that some of these children would not have been missed. But each child that she held briefly in her arms seemed to show her the way back to where he or she had once belonged. And it was but the work of a moment to place the child back in the cradle it had been taken from as if it had never been gone.

The changelings were "removed" a euphemism that surely needs no further explanation. And, in their guise as innocent children, this part of the operation was not always easy for Tamar and Denny.

'I've never seen so many different nurseries in my life,' said Denny when they had finished. 'I never thought I ever would. Life's a funny thing isn't it?'

'I'll never know how we did that,' Tamar said.

'Not without a TARDIS anyway,' said Denny laughing.
But Tamar did not know what a TARDIS was.[*]

'I don't think I want to know,' she continued, therefore, ignoring this. 'We've been messing about in time too much lately.'

At this admission, Denny was temporarily speechless.

'It's a good job you're omnipotent then,' he said eventually.

'This would never have worked otherwise,' she said. 'Not without causing a hideous paradox anyway.'

By which Denny understood that Tamar was now running parallel timelines, as he had done when they went to the Faerie realm, in order to keep recent history in its proper place.

'So, it's as if it never happened then?' he asked – 'In a manner of speaking.'

Tamar just smiled. Denny was smart, but he was never able to get his head around this kind of thing.

'You just don't want to know,' she told him. And to this, at least, Denny was forced to heartily acquiesce.

'It all happened and now it's all been put right – people will remember, I can't help that, but ...'

'You know what,' said Denny. 'Never mind.'

---

[*] Although she could have if she had wanted to – being currently omniscient.

It was strange, Denny thought, from the inside, it had looked like an ordinary, slightly damp cave. But from the outside ... he nudged Tamar.

'Now, don't say it's just wishful thinking or anything,' he said, 'but doesn't that look rather like a spaceship to you?'

'Yes,' said Tamar to Denny's everlasting shock and delight, 'I'd say that's exactly what it looks like. And it explains a lot too.'

'It does?'

'Like the portal. I kept wondering about that. Other realms don't usually have portals, what would be the point? But it's obvious now. It was a transportation device into the ship. And the stones disrupted the magnetic field.'

'And the witches blood?' said Denny.

'What, so there can't be magic and mysticism on other planets?' said Tamar. These guys practically invented a whole new mythology by themselves.'

'That's true,' Denny conceded.

'Besides, there's probably some sensible explanation for it,' she added uncertainly. 'Doesn't blood contain iron?'

'Yes.'

'Well, there you are then,' she said as if this explained everything instead of explaining nothing at all.

'But it's not magic?' he said. 'It's technology. *Alien* technology.' he sounded awed.

'It's ... it's a *kind* of magic,' said Tamar uncertainly. 'I mean, you and I both know what magic really is, it's just knowing something more than everyone else knows. That's quantum that is. It's just not the kind of magic that *we* know. Like the mind control thing. No wonder Faerie magic seemed so ... so ...'

'Alien?'

'Yes.' she looked at the remains of the ship and thought about the Faerie realm that had existed and not existed at the same time inside it. 'The same but different,' she said.

'Well, that makes sense,' said Denny. 'If all life in the universe began at the same point ...'

'They were here too long,' said Tamar. 'That's all. First they adapted and then they began to think like us.'

It occurred to Denny that Tamar was getting metaphysical. And she really wasn't any good at it. She *was* good at making up explanations for things that she really did not understand.[*]

'What time is it?' he asked, deciding to change the subject before she dug herself in any deeper.

'The present,' said Tamar unhesitatingly. 'The timelines have joined back up again now. It's like I told you, it's as if nothing ever happened.'

'So we're back?'

'Well, we've caught up with ourselves anyway.'

'Funny, it didn't seem to take all that long.'

'Well. I may have moved us forward a week or so,' admitted Tamar.

'I never felt a thing,' Denny rubbed his hands together. 'A good day's work,' he said. 'The Faerie Queen is gone, and we've rescued all the kids and we did all that without causing a temporal paradox – right?'

'It's not over,' said Tamar soberly.

'I know that,' snapped Denny coming back to reality. 'Er – what now then?'

'We go home. I want to find out what's been going on. *This* time,' she added.

* * *

'Don't make any sudden moves,' said Stiles as they watched the dragon scrabbling on the tiles. It seemed to be trying to stand up but the floor was too slippery and its legs kept sliding away from it.

'It's a dragon,' said Cindy rather pointlessly. She was trying to hide behind Finvarra, whose chivalry apparently had its limits, and would not let her.

'Yes, stand back,' said Stiles. 'This bears investigating.' And he walked slowly towards it.

---

[*] Which was not to say that she was not usually right. Or at least wrong with more style than people usually are.

'*Investigating*?' said Cindy incredulously. 'Just *kill* it.'

'Do we really have time for this?' snapped Finvarra. You can see that he was getting used to the presence of his god already.

'We may have. Where did it come from, and why?' said Stiles. 'And why is it here, in our home, I mean?'

'Why not just ask it?' said Finvarra. 'Dragons *can* talk.'

'I doubt it has anything to say,' said Stiles.

The dragon raised its head and gave Stiles a malevolent look. 'Wanna go ho-ome,' it whined. 'Ho-ome.'

'Faerie land?' asked Stiles.

'There are no dragons in Faerie land,' said Finvarra. They are … were native to *this* world.'

But the dragon replied. 'Ye-es, ho –ome. Etee, go ho-ome.'

'How did you get here?' demanded Stiles.

'Accident.'

'What happened?' asked Stiles more urgently. 'What accident?'

'Two came, no Faeries, had to leave, make balance. Wanna go Ho-ome. Two left now. Go ho-ome.'

'So, go ho-ome, I mean home, then,' said Stiles.

'What's it talking about?' said Cindy.

'Can't find,' said the dragon. 'Home gone.' And then to everyone's horror, the dragon began to cry. Large hot tears splashed down its snout onto the tiles. Steam rose from the floor as each tear landed. Everyone jumped back quickly.

'It came through when Tamar and Denny entered the Faerie realm,' translated Stiles. 'And now they're back, "two came" "two left." Now he wants to go home but he can't. "Home gone". Which means … Tamar has done it, she's destroyed the Faerie realm and the children are back. It's time to light the lamp.'

He looked at Cindy. 'It doesn't need a wick. It's not an actual lamp, as such – it just looks like one. Think of it as … as a digital storage device for coded genetic information.'

Cindy looked blank.

'It's magic okay?' said Stiles. 'Well, a *kind* of magic anyway.'

'But there *are* no dragons in the Faerie realm,' repeated Finvarra.

'Look,' said Hecaté, 'as the only person currently present who has ever actually *met* a dragon, there is something wrong with this one. Dragons are not like this. All this "me wanna go home" stuff. Dragons are cunning and wise and have a much better vocabulary than many humans have. I actually met one once that wrote beautiful poetry'

'Yes, said Stiles, 'this may be one of the worst things the Faerie Queen did. She took a noble intelligent creature to her realm and turned it into a – a *pet.*'

'That sounds like her right enough,' said Finvarra gloomily. 'A pet dragon – oh yes very stylish.'

'Isn't there anything we can do for it?' asked Cindy looking with less fear now and more pity at the wretched creature sobbing on the floor.

'I fear not,' said Stiles. 'She will have taken it as a baby and raised it this way, it's too old now to be taught any different.'

'Why is there a dragon on my floor?' said a sharp voice from the door.

'I say, I say, I say, why is there a dragon … sorry.' said Denny coming into the room behind her.

'Why *is* there a dragon on the floor?' he said spotting the offending reptile.

'What's it doing there?' snapped Tamar.

'Crying,' observed Denny. 'Why's everyone staring at us?'

'We're just glad to see you,' said Cindy. 'Um …'

'Fine whatever,' said Tamar dismissive of all unnecessary sentiment. 'What's *he* doing here?' she indicated Finvarra and eyed him with no very friendly gaze.

'Er, he's with me,' said Cindy and took his arm to demonstrate.

Denny felt himself give an internal sigh of relief. An unattached Cindy had been too dangerous a thing for his peace of mind. 'I thought he was dead,' he said then realised that this was not perhaps the most tactful remark.

'Ha! You did?' snorted Finvarra.

Denny thought about it. 'No, I guess not. Mere iron wouldn't have worked on *you* would it – you aren't like the others are you? Any more than *she* was?'

'I already *told* you he wasn't dead,' said Cindy. 'At least I thought … Didn't I? She seemed uncertain.

'You might have,' conceded Denny. 'I've been a bit preoccupied lately.'

'If it makes you feel any better,' said Finvarra, 'it bloody hurt. I had to reconstitute myself – took me ages'

'Well,' said Tamar briskly, showing no sign that she had been surprised by *any* of this. 'Back to business. We've got a lot of Faeries to round up.'

'That,' said Stiles triumphantly, 'is the easy part.'

'It is?' Tamar was nonplussed. And for once, she was unable to hide the fact.

'Cindy, get the lamp,' said Stiles.

Cindy did so with alacrity.

Tamar and Denny looked at each other in bewilderment. Denny shrugged. As much as anything, it was surprising to see Stiles retaining control of the group after Tamar had returned. Being in charge while she was gone, well, as long as Denny was not there of course, was perfectly sensible. But they were *back* now, what the hell was going on?

Stiles placed the lamp reverently on a table in front of him and closed his eyes.

'Somebody had better explain all this to me when it's over,' hissed Tamar.

'Shhh,' said Cindy. And Tamar gave her a look that would have melted steel.

'Steady,' muttered Denny taking her hand.

Suddenly there was a *whoosh* and the lamp lighted. From its top, a bright white light streamed filling the room and printing itself on the back of the eyeballs. Everyone closed their eyes and covered their faces and the light steadily got brighter and brighter. Even Tamar felt like her eyelids were melting. Only Stiles seemed unaffected. He opened his eyes, although no one saw him.

Then the air was filled with shrieks, which lasted a few minutes then stopped abruptly as the light went out.

'Cool!' breathed Denny opening his eyes.

Tamar opened her eyes cautiously. 'What the hell was *that*?' she demanded.

'It's over,' said Stiles and collapsed impressively as the gauntlet unwound itself from his central nervous system and fell with a clatter on the floor.

~ Chapter Twenty Six ~

'ARE YOU SURE you want to do this?' asked Denny.

She had already wished him free, in the normal way, making him human again, and his power now came, as before, from the Athame. Stiles was convalescing, as a person will need to do after a close encounter with a god. The gauntlet was on his bedside table, ready to be used again in an emergency. Stiles did not think that anything would ever be *that* much of an emergency. It was now coded to his genetic information now, however, and could not be used by anyone else until he died. Not that anyone else *wanted* to use it though. Even *he* did not want to use it.

Cindy had apparently gone back to her attitude of good natured contempt toward Denny. She had settled Finvarra in, and he had returned her son. The boys were to be brought up together in what was, in the circumstances, as close to an ideal situation as they were going to get. And Hecaté now had two little "nephews" (both identical) to lavish attention on. No kids anywhere had as much stuff to play with – and I do mean anywhere. They even had their very own pet dragon to ride.

Everything was more or less back to normal. Except for Tamar (and the dragon in the garage).

'It's too much power for one person to have,' she said. 'Even *I* think so,'

'You can handle it.' said Denny playing Devil's advocate.

'Maybe,' said Tamar. 'But it's not right. I can't explain it. I don't want to end up like Askphrit.'

'God forbid,' said Denny with feeling. 'But surely the very fact that you feel like that … he trailed off. 'No,' he said. 'It doesn't work like that, does it?'

Tamar smiled enigmatically. She took the Djinn bottle and threw it dramatically into the fireplace where it smashed.

This time it did not come back. [*]

* * *

Tamar had been somewhat mollified to discover, that although technically Stiles had saved the world this time, it had been her actions in the Faerie realm that had made this possible. A joint effort she could live with. And she *had* rescued the children.

Outside, the world was rebuilding. The scars of the recent occupation were already healing over, and soon no one would really believe it had happened at all – except them. Well, with a dragon in the garage and a spaceship in the cellar, how could they forget?

Denny was fascinated by the spaceship and spent hours in the cellar just looking at it.

It made Tamar nervous. Were there not enough maniacs on this planet without there being (possibly) a whole galaxy more of them out there?

'They weren't maniacs to begin with,' Denny pointed out.

'That's supposed to make me feel better is it?' she said. 'Oh, they were okay, until they came here. Must be the water eh?'

'Something in the air,' said Denny waving his arms vaguely.

'Well, we beat them in the end,' said Tamar with satisfaction.

---

[*] Being omnipotent means that you can do *anything*. Even give up being omnipotent.

'And no one will ever know,' said Denny despondently.

'That's Faerie thinking that is,' said Tamar. 'And it's not like you.'

'I wasn't thinking of me,' said Denny.

'There's a big celebration going on next week,' said Tamar changing the subject.

Denny shrugged. 'I don't do parties,' he said. Tamar's face fell.

Denny looked sideways at her. 'You really want to go?' he asked, hiding a smile.

'N-oo, not if you don't. I suppose it …'

'Look, if you *really* want to go,' he gave a theatrical sigh. 'We can go. I'll even buy you a dress.'

She looked worried.

'You can choose it,' he added hurriedly.

She smiled.

'That's settled then,' said Denny.

'It'll do us *all* good,' said Tamar happily.

* * *

'Well, did you ask him?' said Stiles.

'In a manner of speaking,' said Tamar. 'He's coming anyway.'

'Good, we all need some fun, it'll do us good.'

'That's what I said.'

* * *

'How are you feeling mate?'

Stiles sat up in bed. 'Better than I look,' he said, 'which is par for the course these days.' He sighed.

'I hear Tamar "persuaded" you to go to the party.'

'Yeah,' said Denny with a grin.

'Should be a good night.'

'It's about time, that's all I can say,' said Denny.

'Yeah.' They both looked thoughtful.[*]

'Well.'

Men do this when they cannot think of anything to say to each other.[*]

'Well.'

Denny rose to his feet. 'See you later mate. Feel better.'

'Yeah, thanks.'

Denny left.

* * *

Denny had never seen Tamar so excited about a new dress.

'Well, I never *bought* one before,' she said defensively. 'It's not as if I'm going all girly or anything.'

'Nothing wrong with it if you were,' said Denny, who was looking unusually smart himself. He had even shaved. A hitherto unheard of thing.

'Shopping's fun,' admitted Tamar reluctantly.

Tamar had been dragged round every boutique in the city by Cindy on three successive occasions and had been surprised to find that it had indeed been fun. She had even agreed to do it again, to Cindy's delight.

And now she had been in the bathroom "getting ready" for the past two hours. Denny wondered what on earth she could be doing in there. They shared a bathroom, and he knew perfectly well that there was a complete absence of all the usual feminine paraphernalia that he was vaguely aware of women having lying around the bathroom or bedroom. No hairdryer, curling tongs, straightening irons, no makeup, skin cream, hair remover etc.*

Tamar simply did not need all that stuff. So what the hell was she doing in there all that time?

When she finally emerged she looked like she always did, (which was stunning) but Denny was smart enough to know that he should not mention this.

* * *

They had hired a limousine at Finvarra's insistence; he liked to arrive in style, and, since a coach and four was out of the question, a limo was the next best thing.

---

* So much so that Denny was probably the only attached (to a female that is) male in the universe who did not know what it was like to accidentally brush his teeth with hair removing cream or stand on a hot curling iron with bare feet after a shower or find his razor full of mysterious stubble, not his own.

It was a swinging party. Just the sort of thing Tamar liked, with everyone dressed to the nines – and even to the tens in some cases. Cindy had dressed properly this time, which was a relief to everyone. They had all heard the story from Finvarra, who told it with great gusto at every opportunity until Cindy made him stop.

It was being held outdoors, (presumably to make the point that the Faeries were gone, and they now damn well could if they wanted to) and the crowd that parted as Tamar stepped out of the limo behind Denny was immense and oddly silent.

As she stood in the vacuum created by a thousand people standing back and falling silent, she began to get a funny feeling. Then suddenly a huge cheer went up. Tamar looked around her, bewildered.

A distinguished looking man approached her. She did not recognise him, but his medallion proclaimed him to be the City's Mayor.

She hesitated then curtsied.

'Tamar Black?' the mayor asked her.

'Er, yes, your honour,' she said. Although at that moment, she could not have sworn to it.

'Although nothing would be enough to thank you for the return of this city's children and the restoration of our freedom,' he began. 'We – that is – the people, would like to present you with this small token of our unending esteem and gratitude.' And he pressed a small golden item into her unresisting hands.

She looked at it in shock. It was a small representation of a flaming sword. On the pedestal beneath were inscribed her name and the words *"Protector Of The People"*. She gazed around at the expectant faces all staring at her. Her eyes caught Denny's and he shrugged.

'It was all their idea,' he said. 'I never told anyone anything.'

Someone in the crowd, (there's always one) shouted, 'Speech, speech.' And the rest of the crowd took up the cry.

She looked back at the tiny sword, she read the inscription, and suddenly she began to cry.

'I never … had, 'she begun, 'I never expected … I – I … no one ever thanked me before … thank you.'

This seemed to be enough, which was just as well, since at this point she completely broke down. The crowd began to cheer, and Denny came forward to rescue her.

'You *knew*, didn't you?' she hissed as he piloted her away.

'Oh yes,' he said.

'You tricked me.'

'No one else could have,' he told her. She silently conceded to this.

'I was wrong about people,' she said. 'I never thought …'

'That people could be gracious?' said Denny.

'Yes. I was wrong.' she looked down at her little sword. 'Very wrong. It's the nicest thing I ever got,' she said.

'So far,' said Denny, 'at least I hope …'

'What are you going on about?'

Denny fished in his pocket, brought out a little blue box, and snapped it open. Inside was a diamond ring.

'Only if you get down on one knee this time,' she said.

Denny knelt down to Tamar's surprise. 'Tamar,' he said. 'Will you marry me?'

'And if the world gets taken over by aliens or wizards or dragons?' she said.

'Will you?' he said insistently, 'even if it does?'

'Well, when you put it like that,' she said. 'Yes.'

Epilogue

Meanwhile, in a galaxy far far away... ™

'I don't care what he said ... there's no such thing as aliens.'

'What do you call that then?' said Mixpryt,' thrusting his fellow astronomer's eye to the crystoscope

'Wow!'

'I told you,'

'Nice planet, very lush. Lot's of CO_2 .'

'Yeah, so go and tell General Lurtz that we've found a new home world.'

'What about the *aliens*?' He said this with a degree of awe.

Mixpryt gave his colleague a look that said, "You are not paid to think". 'What about them?' he said. 'Look at them, all milling around inefficiently. They need properly organising if you ask me. Anyway, I doubt there's anyone down there who could stand up to twelve of us together, let alone the invasion force that the high command has put together.'

'Seems a shame,' said the assistant astronomer.

'Ha!' said Mixpryt. 'They won't know what hit 'em.'

'Oh, I think they *will* know what's hit them,' said the other. 'I mean when tens of thousands pounds of ...'

'It's a *saying*,' said Mixpryt impatiently.

'Really, what does it mean then?'

'Look – go and inform the General like a good chap will you? And then sort out the magic rings. Have us there in jig time.'

'What kind of magic do you think the aliens have?' asked the unfortunate assistant astronomer, who really did have a talent for putting his flipper in it.

'Don't be silly,' said Mixpryt. 'Everyone knows that aliens don't have magic. Only proper people like *us* have magic.'

He gave this some thought and added. 'Only don't tell the General about it. He won't be able to cope if we tell him it's all done by magic. *He* thinks it's some sort of *technology*'

He slotted a new crystal ball into the crystoscope and resumed his study of the fascinating planet he had found. He found himself getting quite interested in the goings on down there. It was a bit like watching an opera at the coliseum (only without the funny hats) or the moving pictures that so many *ordinary* people liked to watch at home. This, he suspected, was better. It would be better still if there were more explosions. 'Now that,' he thought, '*would* be entertainment.'

*

On the world that Mixpryt was watching, there was a girl watching the sky. A girl with a flaming sword. A flaming sword that said "*Protector Of The People*"

Well, it's a *kind* of magic.

THE SIXTH ADVENTURE IN THE TAMAR BLACK
SERIES – COMING SOON!

Tamar Black – Anything But Ordinary

Is Denny Sanger the sexiest man in the world?

This – and other crucial questions – are now being asked by the world's press (and secret government agencies)

Since saving the world from the Faeries, Tamar, Denny and Co are now famous. Reporters are now camping out on the doorstep twenty four hours a day. And who are the two strange men in the blacked out car?

And, as if that was not enough, Tamar is having so much fun going shopping and painting her nails that it is driving Denny absolutely crazy trying to convince her that she is …

ANYTHING BUT ORDINARY

As the wedding approaches, and the strain is beginning to tell on Tamar and Denny, their friends are beginning to wonder if they will make it to the church (this time)?

And then they discover that they are not the only ones out there saving the world.

SCI 'ON _ The Shadow Worlds

The first book in the SCI 'ON Trilogy

Whenever a decision is taken that is of significance to the world, the world divides and two alternate futures are created. In the beginning, there was only one world. That world we name SCI 'ON. All other worlds that sprang from it, we name the shadow worlds. Some believe SCI 'ON is the only real world and that all others are mere reflections, hence the name. Others believe that all the alternate worlds are equally real and important – however they may have come into being.

Whatever the case, one thing is certain. If SCI 'ON itself – the cradle of creation– were to be destroyed, all other worlds would cease to exist. For SCI'ON is the mainspring and without it, the shadow worlds would have no point of origin.

Johnny Hammond is not your ordinary computer nerd. He has the makings of a hero. When a mysterious man shows him the way To SCI 'ON, Johnny becomes obsessed. And only he can find a way to get there through the myriad shadow worlds that stand in his way. But someone doesn't want him to get there.

From earliest childhood, Ryan and Kai have been best friends. The fact that they come from separate universes is not allowed to stand in their way.

As they grow up, they realise that this ability to travel between the worlds is no mere coincidence, as their ultimate destiny unfolds.

About the Author

Nicola Rhodes often can't remember where she lives so she lives inside her own head most of the time, where even if you do get lost, it's still okay.

She has met many interesting people inside her own head and eventually decided to introduce the rest of the world to them, in the hopes that they would stop bothering her and let her sleep.

She has been doing this for ten years now but they still won't leave her alone.

She wrote this book for fun and does not care if you take away a moral lesson from it or not.

You have her full permission to read whatever you wish into this work of fiction. As she says herself:

"Just because I wrote this book, doesn't mean I know anything about it."

www.ingramcontent.com/pod-product-compliance
Lightning Source LLC
Chambersburg PA
CBHW020600250626
47154CB00004B/1302